THE FLETCHER LEGACY

As president of the family paper mills, Leslie was determined to carry on the proud Fletcher name. But she hadn't counted on woodsman Gage Preston stepping into her life. Pollution of the environment was Gage's main concern, and the Fletcher mills were his key target. But it was his passionate embrace that filled Leslie with the most fear. How could she protect the mills when her greatest enemy had made her feel — for the first time — so wonderfully and ecstatically like a woman.

JILLIAN DAGG

THE FLETCHER LEGACY

Complete and Unabridged

LINFORD
Leicester

First published in 1984 in the
United States of America

First Linford Edition
published 2004

British Library CIP Data

Dagg, Jillian
    The Fletcher legacy.—Large print ed.—
Linford romance library
1. Love stories
2. Large type books
I. Title II. Wildman, Faye
813.9'14 [F]

ISBN 1–84395–306–4

Published by
F. A. Thorpe (Publishing)
Anstey, Leicestershire

Set by Words & Graphics Ltd.
Anstey, Leicestershire
Printed and bound in Great Britain by
T. J. International Ltd., Padstow, Cornwall

This book is printed on acid-free paper

To Nancy Jackson for making my writing career a reality, and Leslie Wainger and Frances Jalet for their continuing help and belief in me. Thank you.

1

Gage Preston loved the stillness of the forest. The previous night's rain dripped through the trees and matched the crunch of his footsteps over the undergrowth. He sniffed the damp, pine-scented air and wished he didn't also have to inhale the faint sulfur odor of the Fletcher Paper mill.

He imagined what it must have been like here when his ancestors first settled the area. The forest would have been completely intact, and the inlet and waterways clear and undisturbed by industry. But Gage didn't like to complain. Preston Falls was still a good place to be.

As he trekked along the earthy path to his cottage, he felt proud of his handbuilt home. On the veranda, he kicked the mud from his boots and loosened the laces. After stepping from the leather work boots, he pushed open the wooden door and walked across the thick rust carpet that contrasted well with the brown kitchen tiles.

Coffee was perking in the pot as Gage had left it before his morning walk. He took bacon and eggs from the refrigerator and began to fry up his breakfast, wondering at the slight disquiet within him this morning. It was almost as if something intangible had disturbed him earlier than his usual seven A.M. wakeup and dragged him out of bed into the British Columbia rainforest.

He shrugged his broad shoulders to release the tension in his six-foot frame. Something was wrong, yet outside the window everything looked the same. The snowy mountain peaks towered above the evergreen slopes. The spiral of white smoke from Fletcher Paper puffed against the blue sky.

As Gage turned his bacon and eggs onto a plate and sat down at the table to eat, there was a rap at the front door.

'Come in,' Gage called. It was Peter Slater, the union head at the paper mill. Gage waved a slice of toast at him. 'Want some?'

'Sure,' Peter said, waving a newspaper, trying to outdo the toast, 'but get a load of this.'

Gage indicated where Peter should sit. Then he looked at the newspaper headline: *Paul Fletcher Dead.*

'Shoot. I knew there was something wrong.' Gage swallowed his toast and smoothed the paper to read the text of the article. 'I woke up this morning with a peculiar sensation.'

'You and your sixth sense.' Peter helped himself to half a slice of toast, and added strawberry jam from the jar. 'The mill is in an uproar, but I don't think it'll change anything.'

Gage looked thoughtful as his eyes scanned the rest of the story. 'Are you sure?'

Peter got his meaning. 'You think this might be an opportunity, Gage?'

'Why not? We've been after Fletcher

Paper to increase the pollution controls on the mill for a year.'

'And we still need safer working conditions.'

'Which you'll get if they update the equipment,' Gage pointed out. 'What do you think?'

'Well, with Fletcher out of the way, we might be able to get somewhere.'

'Who's taking over?'

'His daughter.'

'A woman?'

Peter raised gray eyebrows. 'Now, Gage. Don't let my Molly hear you say that. She's all for women's lib.'

Gage laughed. 'I didn't mean it that way. I think this is too much of a chance to miss, Peter. His daughter will be vulnerable at first, won't she?'

Peter's gray eyes crinkled. 'I like the word vulnerable.'

'So do I. I've been longing for the day when I would have the upper hand over Fletcher Paper.'

'Only one thing, Gage.' Peter turned serious as he ran his fingers through his wavy gray hair. 'I don't mind you fighting for a better environment. It's just that this whole town depends on Fletcher for its livelihood. I don't want the jobs jeopardized in any way. Got me?'

Gage nodded, recognizing the hard-line edge in his friend that made him a good bargaining head for the union. 'I won't go that far. Everyone wants a clean water system.'

'I know.' Peter nodded. 'It's all a paradox.'

Gage agreed. 'My log salvaging business needs companies like Fletcher as much as you do. I can't afford to have them close down.'

'As long as you recognize that, Gage.' Peter stood up, stuffing his hands in the pockets of his faded jeans. 'So what do you propose to do?'

'I'll go visit Fletcher's daughter in Vancouver.' Gage grinned. 'Get her before she's settled in.'

'Good idea,' Peter said. 'You might even enjoy yourself. Cliff Daniels, the general manager at the mill, says she's a doll.'

'Then what am I waiting for?'

★   ★   ★

Brass trim glinted in the pale sunshine as the rich wood coffin hung poised over freshly dug earth. Leslie Fletcher felt detached as she watched the proceedings, and recalled the frantic events of the last few days. First there had been the evening phone call to tell her about her father's heart attack, followed by the long tense wait at the hospital and then finally the news that Paul Fletcher was dead.

Leslie's velvet brown eyes slipped over the people surrounding the grave. Frank Lehman, Paul Fletcher's personal advisor, his sleek black hair plastered to his head, his black suit and overcoat immaculate, stood next to her mother. Frank wouldn't show his grief, but Leslie knew he would be feeling it.

Fresh out of the university at twenty-four he had come to work for her father. In his early forties now, Frank had been a faithful worker and a good friend to the family. Leslie had even dated him a few times, finding him a pleasant, if pedantic, companion. She had often wondered why he had never married because he would have made a steady husband. Instead, he was married to his work or, more correctly, he was devoted to Fletcher Paper.

Her glance moved to her mother. Caroline Fletcher's aging face was crinkled with strain beneath her black veil, the collar of her black fur coat framing her thin neck. She was a slim, perfectly dressed, elegant little woman, not at all the type of woman one would imagine to complement Paul Fletcher's dashing image, but Leslie was sure that Caroline was the only person in the world who had truly known Paul Fletcher, the man. As far as Leslie knew, they'd had a good marriage, but Leslie felt it was because Caroline had never put up a fight. Paul had needed a woman at home to renew his vigor in the marketplace, and Caroline had bowed to his wishes. Whenever Leslie had questioned her mother about the weakness of living in Paul Fletcher's shadow, Caroline had always shrugged and said, 'I love him.'

Leslie couldn't believe that loving a man meant you lost all your self-respect. That was one of the reasons she was still single at twenty-eight. If her father was any indication, men seemed to like women they could bend to their will. Of course, there was another reason she wasn't married. She had never found a man to stir her senses. Love was elusive, like the strains of a song that refused to form a whole tune in her mind.

Her eyes traced the line of other mourners. Most of them were employees of Fletcher who had served her father for years. For a wealthy, powerful man, Paul Fletcher had few friends. Everyone sensed that he had been his own person. He hadn't let anyone near. Including his own daughter, Leslie thought wryly, her gaze resting on a man she didn't recognize. He stood, solid as a rock, his eyes trained on the coffin.

Did she imagine the cynical twist to the man's firm lips? Who was he? He was definitely not an employee, but he could be a business associate.

The man raised his head until Leslie was looking at him face on. He was rough hewn and tanned, his curly hair mostly dark blond but with lighter wisps lit by the streaky sunlight. His hands were stuffed into the pockets of his navy trenchcoat open over a silvery gray suit, the clothes covering his large frame with easy assurance. And yet Leslie was under the impression that he would be more at home in jeans and a work shirt. There was a sensation of muscular power, held in by the comformity of style.

His narrowed eyes recognized her scrutiny and he allowed himself his own in return: following the line of her neat black hat, covering a curly halo of chestnut hair; black veil, obscuring her features; and black jersey wool dress, peeking from a slim matching coat.

As the man's eyes roamed down her long slender legs in charcoal hose to the tips of her black leather high heels, Leslie began to feel a little awkward. Thinking that one day he might be one of her business associates, and using the gesture to avoid further staring, Leslie moved her lips in a greeting that thanked him for attending the funeral.

The man acknowledged her greeting by exhaling a short breath that puffed like smoke into the chilly air.

Experiencing a response she couldn't pin down, Leslie dropped her glance. Paul Fletcher's coffin was disappearing from view, and a sudden vision of her father edged in: six-foot, dynamic, with steel gray hair, larger than life. Was he really in that box? If someone had jumped up and declared the funeral a joke, she would have trusted him. From the moment she had heard of her father's death she hadn't believed it. Men like Paul Fletcher didn't die. She had supposed that he was immortal.

Tears were trickling down Caroline's lined face, and when Frank handed her a crisp white linen handkerchief she began to sniff discreetly. Leslie couldn't cry. Conflicting feelings for her father made her feel remote, almost numb.

She turned away from her mother's side now that the service was over and walked across the grass to the waiting limousine, enjoying the motion after standing for so long. When a hand on her arm made her turn abruptly, her perfectly painted coral lips opened questioningly.

'Miss Fletcher?' The male voice was low and husky.

'Yes.' Leslie recognized the man she had been staring at earlier. At closer inspection she saw that his nose was well-shaped, his top lip firm and straight giving way to a slight sensuality in his bottom lip. His jaw was tough and lean, but she supposed the strongest feature was his eyes — a deep, dark blue that pierced through long brown lashes. The sun heightened the blondish curls and there was a smooth texture to his golden skin.

He smiled, showing a row of strong white teeth. 'My name's Gage Preston. I'd like to speak to you at a convenient moment.'

'Go ahead.' Leslie shrugged, expecting another glib condolence. From the corner of her eye she saw that her mother was still at the graveside with Frank clinging to her arm.

When nothing came from the man, she urged, 'What did you want?'

'In private,' Gage Preston suggested. 'I want to discuss business.'

'This is hardly the time,' she told him with an edge of impatience. 'I've just buried my father. Maybe in a few days.'

'I haven't got a few days,' the man said in a low firm voice. 'How about your home?'

'I don't invite strange men to my

home, Mr. Preston.'

'Then your office?'

Leslie watched him through the small black dots of her veil. 'You're persistent, Mr. Preston. I can't think of anything that can't wait until Monday when I take over the presidency of Fletcher Paper.'

'Then you are taking over?'

A faint smile touched Leslie's coral lips. 'You knew that.'

Gage nodded, acknowledging her smile. 'Yes, I did. I read of your father's heart attack, and the fact that you had inherited the responsibility of Fletcher Paper. I won't take too much of your time.'

Leslie considered him again. Why not get it over with? After all, she had enough work looming on her desk for Monday morning without adding Gage Preston to the pile. 'Okay,' she agreed at last. 'I'll meet you in my office.'

Gage inclined his head. 'Fine. I have a car.' He pointed to a silver gray Porsche.

Leslie eyed the sleek car and she eyed the man. She tried to search her

13

memory to remember if she had heard of Gage Preston, but she hadn't. She was certainly not going in a car with a strange man. Her family was rich. There was such a thing as kidnapping.

'I have my own transportation,' she said. 'I'll see you there.'

'Half an hour,' he said.

'Half an hour.' She nodded, and watched him stride to the Porsche. He climbed in, closed the door and drove off with a roar of the powerful engine. The man was like the car, Leslie concluded, her glance on the flashing red brake lights as the Porsche slowed at the cemetery exit. With a shrug, she looked to where her mother was slowly moving along with Frank.

'Come on, Mother,' she said. 'You must get home. It's all over.'

*   *   *

The air inside the limousine was aromatic with the scent of expensive leather. Breathing a sigh of relief to see

14

the car containing her mother and Frank move off, Leslie gave instructions to her own chauffeur to take her downtown.

Pensively, chin in palm, she sat gazing out the window. Usually the mountains that set the city of Vancouver in an oasis were shrouded with mist, but today the sun picked out the snow-capped peaks and sent shadows spiraling down the fir-covered slopes. The silvery wake of a barge broke the blueness of the Pacific, acting as a backdrop to the downtown high-rise skyline and the Friday bustle of crowds.

The play of sunlight on the office-block windows reminded Leslie of the way Gage Preston's hair had shone in the streaky rays out at the cemetery. She felt a flutter of anticipation at the thought of seeing him again. The feeling was so unusual that Leslie placed her hand against her stomach. Most of her dates brought her no thrill at all. The men themselves might have been robots, wound up to act as escorts, because it was expected that Leslie Fletcher be seen with men, and men liked to be seen with Leslie Fletcher.

She was envied and sought after because she was rich. People didn't know of the loneliness and the constant fight to live up to her father's standards. Leslie glanced at her pale coral fingernails, long and exquisitely manicured. No longer did she chew them nervously. She was now the child Paul Fletcher had wanted. A chip off the old Fletcher block. She was unawakened, hard of heart, more like her father than she ever dared admit. Was that why he had left her the responsibility of Fletcher Paper?

Refusing to let the prospect of the presidency weigh too heavily on her shoulders, Leslie sat upright, gathering her black leather clutch purse as the limousine slid to a halt outside the Fletcher Tower. The steel and glass building was a manmade landmark in a city dominated by natural landmarks. As long as the building stood, her father's name was still a positive force.

Thick caramel-colored carpet and her father's secretary, Julie Wells, greeted Leslie as the elevator doors swished open to the executive offices.

Julie stood up, her slim blue dress hugging voluptuous curves while the color complemented feathered blonde hair. Slim legs teetered above black patent heels. 'Miss Fletcher . . . ' she began.

Leslie smiled. 'I know, there's someone here to see me.' Leslie walked toward the black leather doors with the gold inscription: *Paul Fletcher, President.*

Julie hovered behind her. 'I gave him coffee. I didn't know if it was really wise. I wasn't expecting you.'

'That's fine, Julie.' Leslie saw her own name in gold, as it would be one day, before she pushed open the doors. She tugged off the black hat and veil to let her tangled chestnut brown curls free.

Gage Preston stood with his back to

the open caramel-colored drapes, the sea and mountains acting as his scenery. He'd tossed his navy trench-coat over one of the worn amber leather chairs, and he seemed quite at home as he drank coffee from a white porcelain cup.

Leslie's eyes met his, and she felt the same jab of anticipation that she had experienced in the limousine.

Gage lifted the cup. 'Your secretary kindly gave me coffee.'

'So she said. As long as there's some left for me.' Leslie moved forward with graceful strides despite her high heels and the fact that her legs felt quite weak from the man's presence. She placed her purse and hat on the desk and slipped out of the black coat. 'It was cold standing out there.'

'It was,' Gage agreed, making no move to assist her as if sensing that she would rather do everything herself.

Leslie smoothed her black jersey dress over her hips, aware of Gage's eyes on her full breasts, flat stomach and long legs. She was used to men looking at her. The male sex sensed a mystery and tried to conquer it. But Gage's look was more assessing than the usual blatant stares. His blue eyes probed right through her.

Leslie poured herself coffee from the tall white porcelain pot. 'Funerals aren't my favorite Friday afternoon entertainment. I don't suppose they're yours either.'

'Not really.' Gage gave her a slight smile.

'Oh well, only one father, only one funeral and now it's over.' Leslie returned Gage's intense gaze. Handsome wasn't the word to describe him, she thought. This man should be preserved in granite. He was so forceful, so strong, that she felt stunned by him. Her father had always looked large and a part of this office. Gage Preston also fitted in.

She sipped from her cup, eyeing him over the white rim, thinking that they couldn't stand here for the rest of the day looking at each other. 'Well?'

'I expected you to be less composed,' Gage said abruptly.

'I thought I was a nervous wreck.' She smiled, showing small even teeth. 'But I don't display my feelings in public. You learn that kind of thing when you're rich, Mr. Preston.'

Leslie could discern a slight discomfort in the man's large frame, but it wasn't noticeable when he spoke. 'Then you'll probably make a good president.'

'Who knows,' Leslie said dramatically, her innermost fears rushing to the surface. 'Look at this place.' Her arm formed an arc against the muted earthy colors of the gilt-framed paintings on the wall. 'Do I fit in here?'

Gage's mouth curved unwillingly as if enjoying her cynical humor. He used her question to his advantage, giving her another sweeping blue look, resting a long time on her breasts and full mouth before meeting her glance again. 'Actually, the surroundings quite suit you.'

Leslie was serious. 'Do you really think so?'

'Yes, I really think so.'

'Good, because I'm going to have to fit in. I don't have any choice.' Leslie put down her cup, realizing that she was losing control. Her emotions were bursting forth and she felt powerless to stop them. She picked up a photograph of herself from the long oak desk. Well-shaped dark brown eyebrows were raised slightly over velvet brown eyes hinting at mischievousness, while her mouth was set in a little pout. Brown hair with tints of red cascaded in shiny waves to her shoulders, and full breasts were emphasized by a low-cut rust velvet gown. 'I was twenty-five when this was taken.' Leslie let Gage see the picture. 'My father insisted I have the photograph done so he could put it on his desk. I made faces at the photographer.'

Gage took the photograph from her. 'For what reason did you think your father wanted to have the picture?' he asked, taking a good look before replacing the frame on the desk.

'Who knew my father's motives,' Leslie said.

'I gather you weren't close to your father.'

'Not particularly.' Leslie sighed.

Gage pointed to the photograph. 'How many years have passed since then?'

'Three.' Leslie suddenly realized that this man was making her vulnerable. The only other man in her life who had ever done that was her father. And yet she used to pretend she didn't care. So much rejection had turned her emotions inward, making her appear cynical.

'You'll be a young president,' Gage said. 'But I'm sure you'll cope. You've probably been groomed for the position since birth.'

'Probably,' Leslie agreed, finally getting a hold over herself.

Gage seemed to sense that she regained her composure. He drained his coffee cup before replacing it carefully on the wooden tray. 'Don't you want to know why I'm here?'

'Of course.'

'I'm from Preston Falls.'

Leslie didn't like the assumption that she would immediately know what that meant, and she was in no mood for fooling around, especially with a man who affected her emotions so skittishly. 'Well, goodie,' she jeered.

Gage raised a dark blond eyebrow. 'Have you heard of it?'

'Yes, I've heard of it. We have a small paper mill there. Is it a coincidence that your name is Preston?'

'The Falls were named after one of my ancestors.'

'So you're a true, blue British Columbian.' Her voice lilted teasingly to hide the edge of frustration.

Gage's mouth firmed, making the sensual bottom lip straighten stubbornly. 'You could say that.'

Leslie's long brown lashes fluttered. There was definitely something in his bold blue glance that excited her. She had never met a man with such charisma. To antagonize him would thwart her chances of getting to know him better.

'I'm a true, blue British Columbian as well.' She smiled and stretched out her hand in a friendly gesture. 'Shall we begin again, Mr. Preston?'

As he took her hand, Leslie had to stifle the urge to draw him closer. His fingers were rough, but with a strength that told her he wouldn't take any nonsense. Maybe she had been right with her first impression of him. He seemed like a man who worked at manual labor, and now that she knew he was from a northern Canadian community, she could be correct. 'I'm pleased to meet you,' she said.

Gage pulled his hand away slowly. 'And I'm pleased to meet you, Miss Fletcher.'

She nearly said, 'Call me Leslie,' but checked herself. He might know that she thought he was attractive if she became too forward. She went to stand behind her father's large desk. 'Well then, do you want to tell me why you're here?'

Gage slid his hands into his pockets, and his look was thoughtful as if he were weighing the situation. 'First of all I want to say that I'm sorry about your father's sudden death. It must have been a shock.'

'It was a bit,' Leslie agreed, her fingers idly toying with a carved cigarette box. Everything was in order as if her father had left the place one afternoon, as if he'd never been taken ill and died. She felt tears welling. Oh no, not in front of him. Leslie moved to look out the window, and blinked away the spilling moisture.

There was a long silence in which she knew Gage was watching her. Finally he spoke softly. 'I'm sorry. I'll come back another day. Would Monday suit you better?'

As the ache of her father's death penetrated, relief flooded her that he was going to leave. 'Please.' Leslie turned around but she couldn't stop the tears.

Gage reached in his top pocket and drew out a crisp blue handkerchief. 'Here.'

A fragrance, fresh as the forest, reached Leslie's nostrils as she shook out the handkerchief and blotted her eyes. 'I'm being silly.' She handed the crumpled handkerchief back to him.

He tucked it in his pocket. 'You're not being silly. It was a little presumptuous of me to push this meeting.'

'How about eleven, Monday morning,' Leslie suggested huskily. 'I have a board meeting first.'

Gage picked up his coat and hung it from his shoulder. 'Eleven's fine,' he said, disappearing through the black doors.

Leslie stared at the doors for a long time before sinking into her father's huge leather chair. She buried her face in her hands, wiping away stray tears. Her father was dead, and she was president of the company, a position that would take her months to comprehend before she felt at ease. Then a thought struck her. Was she really crying for her father, or was she crying because she didn't have a man like Gage Preston? He was her fantasy man, yet he might not be real. He had entered her life quickly, and had gone just as fast.

Agitated, Leslie punched the intercom button to summon Julie Wells.

'Yes, Miss Fletcher,' Julie said, standing in the doorway.

Leslie forced a smile for the secretary who was now hers. 'Would you find something out about a man named Gage Preston?'

'Yes, Miss Fletcher.'

'Thank you, Julie. I want the information for Monday morning.'

'I'll try.'

When Julie had gone, Leslie reached in her purse and pulled out a wad of tissues. She blew her nose, then stood up and walked around the office.

She could feel her father's presence. When she was little, his office had been in an older block, and she had often gone to wait for him with her mother. The desk and chairs had been the same, though, and she used to play with his cigarettes in the carved box, his gold pen . . . She opened the drawer and rifled through the papers, pens, paper-clips . . . her fingers closed around a plastic pill bottle, and she drew it out. 'Take three times a day, or for discomfort.' Discomfort? Had Paul Fletcher been feeling heart pain for a long time?

About a month ago, her father had called her into his office. He had stood with his hands clasped behind his back, his characteristic pose, while he stared out the window.

'It's a nice view,' he had commented.

Leslie had laughed. It wasn't often that her father noticed the environment around him.

Turning around slowly, Paul Fletcher had said, 'Leslie, if anything happens to me, I want you to take on Fletcher Paper.'

She had laughed again. 'That'll be the day.'

Leslie tossed the pink and blue pills into the drawer and closed it. That day had come sooner than she thought.

2

Home at last. Leslie eagerly discarded the black funeral dress for jeans and a knit gold sweater. But her mood was somber as she ate a green salad while lounging in one of her apricot velvet armchairs. Even the panoramic view from her apartment window didn't thrill her tonight. The flashing neon sign, giving the time and temperature, irritated her, and the Grouse Mountain ski lift, tracking its lighted way through the dusk, reminded her that other people weren't alone.

She supposed she should be with her mother. Caroline hadn't liked the fact that Leslie had taken a separate car from the funeral, but she had been too distraught to argue. But now Leslie wanted to be alone. She wasn't sure if it was her father's death that had caused this off-balance sensation, or the meeting with Gage Preston.

Gage floated into her memory. What was he like beneath his rock-hard exterior? Was he married? Probably, knowing my luck, she thought wryly.

Leslie placed her empty salad dish on a teak side table and stood up, her bare toes pressing into the deep ivory carpet. Her apartment was so perfect. Pristine cream drapes flowed at the windows framing the velvet sofa and chairs, the apricot coloring dotted with triangles and circles of pastel green and blue velvet cushions. Slashes of bright color on canvas hung against the ivory walls. In the bedroom, the color scheme was similar, centered by a queen-size bed covered with oyster silk. The bathroom was huge with a gray marble vanity and bathtub large enough for two. Even the primrose yellow in the kitchen had been chosen with care. A decor to make an impression on her father.

'Ah, this is nice,' Paul Fletcher had said when he'd been invited to the penthouse suite for the first time, 'if you must live alone. This is how I envision it.'

Everything for her father. Leslie's entire life had revolved around Paul Fletcher. Other men had been weak in comparison — except Gage Preston. Gage seemed to have Paul Fletcher's power and presence without her father's ruthlessness.

Caroline had once told Leslie that Paul wasn't really ruthless; he just didn't know how to show his feelings. But Leslie hadn't found that plausible. Surely, if that were true, she would have seen through him and known if he'd loved her. As it was, he might never have cared. She was a possession, to be plied with money and clothes, and to be used to carry on the Fletcher name.

Unable to endure the claustrophobic effect of her apartment any longer, Leslie put a navy suede bomber jacket over her jeans, pushed her feet into socks and navy boots and stuffed her door keys into her pocket.

She knew it wasn't really wise to walk

alone on English Bay Beach at night, but she needed exercise, fresh air and a change of scenery. She might not have felt close to her father in life, but now that he was gone, a void was opening. Her fingers clenched into her palms in her pockets.

I'm gonna miss you, Dad, she thought. I never dreamed I would ever miss you.

As her leather soles crunched on the stony beach, the ocean crashed to shore, and she realized how life went on interminably, even without her father. Tears filled her eyes. Why hadn't she felt this sadness at the funeral? Perhaps she was having a delayed reaction.

Containing the tears, she sat down on a driftwood log and stared out to sea to watch a ship cruise the horizon. Fletcher Paper was a big responsibility, and right now she wasn't sure she could cope. The hysteria she had felt when she first entered her father's office this afternoon returned to haunt her. She had let her emotions go in front of

Gage Preston but, although a little embarrassed in retrospect, she knew he would understand how she felt.

A pebble splashed and darted over the water in front of her, and she glanced around to see what had caused it. To her surprise, Gage Preston was squatting a few feet from her, wearing old jeans and a black turtleneck beneath a tailored black leather jacket.

Leslie raised an eyebrow. 'Is it Monday morning already?'

Gage's smile was white in the dark. 'No.'

'Are you staying near here?'

'Across the street.' He indicated the row of high-rise apartments on the other side of the road. 'Do you live near here?'

'Over there.' Leslie waved her arm in the direction of her own high-rise.

Gage straightened and rested his foot on the log. 'Are you feeling the loss tonight?'

He was perceptive. Leslie shrugged. 'My father was the type of man who was larger than life.'

'I never met him.'

She looked at him curiously. 'I was under the impression that you had.'

'I just know a lot about him,' he clarified, 'being that one of your mills is in Preston Falls.'

Leslie heard the emphasis on his last sentence and kicked a stone from its nest in the damp sand. 'I presume what you know isn't favorable.'

'Not particularly.'

'You're not alone,' she admitted. 'I'm not even sure if I liked him. It's just that — he was my father. This afternoon I found some heart pills in his desk. He had probably been in pain for some time.'

'And he never told you?'

She shook her head. 'Or my mother, apparently. He didn't overdose on talking about himself.'

'I'm sorry.'

Leslie laughed harshly. 'I doubt if you are. I think the only person who is genuinely upset is my mother.'

'Then what are you feeling?'

'Just a little melancholy, Mr. Preston.' Leslie felt she had talked too much, maybe been too revealing. She stood up and brushed down her jeans. 'I guess I'd better get home.'

Gage lowered his foot, and the pebbly beach slithered beneath his boots. 'Why don't you let me buy you some ice cream?'

Leslie smiled at this unexpected offer. 'At this time of year?'

'Who cares? I've been pigging out in that ice cream parlor over on the corner. The staff's getting suspicious because I'm always alone.'

Having ice cream seemed like a lovely, frivolous thing to do. Soon enough Leslie would be back at work with all the problems of Fletcher Paper to worry about.

'Okay,' she agreed.

Gage put out his hand and Leslie let his fingers weave warmly around hers. He swung her arm slightly as they walked up the beach.

What am I doing? Leslie thought as they strolled from the beach over the grass mound to the road. *I don't know this man from Adam. He's a complete stranger.* But he had a definite appeal. There was an odd sense, as if they had been destined to meet. Leslie had never felt such an affinity with a man.

Heads turned when they entered the ice cream parlor, and Leslie felt conspicuous as she took her place with her back to the wall. She was used to expensive restaurants with low lighting where the waiters knew her by name.

Gage sat down opposite, and in the strong yellow light he looked large, his dark clothing setting off his golden tan and fair curly hair to advantage.

They were given menus, and Gage ordered a hot fudge sundae and coffee. Leslie, to spare herself the decision from the many varieties, ordered the same. She glanced out of the window, to the darkened bay. Headlights from the cars along the shoreline road kept up a steady stream.

'You seem uneasy,' Gage said.

Leslie dragged her glance back to him. She couldn't very well tell him that his choice of restaurant wasn't her usual haunt. She didn't want to appear like a snob because she had always prided herself on the fact that she wasn't.

'I'm fine,' she told him.

'If you want to talk about the funeral or your father to let off steam, go ahead,' Gage said as they were served coffee.

'Didn't I do that this afternoon?' Leslie asked, turning her cup on the saucer.

'Was that letting off steam? I thought that was a natural reaction for a woman who'd just buried her father.'

'I'm not the emotional type; for me that was letting off steam,' Leslie admitted, wondering what it was about Gage that made her drop her defenses.

Their sundaes were brought to them, and Leslie picked up the long-handled spoon.

Gage dug into his concoction of chocolate sauce, nuts and ice cream. 'Come on, eat up,' he urged.

Leslie tasted the smooth mixture of sauce and ice cream. The sundae was delicious. She ate another scoop. 'This is fantastic. Guaranteed to put on pounds and pounds.'

'You could do with it.'

'How do you know? I might have to jog halfway around Vancouver every morning to keep my figure.'

Gage grinned. 'A man needs something to hold on to.'

It was a blatant, flirtatious remark. Leslie felt her face flush. 'Who says you'll ever be allowed to hold on?' she asked huskily.

'I didn't think I could make you blush.' Gage looked amused. 'That'll be something to tell them at home.'

Leslie felt rage catch in her throat, and she put down her spoon. 'Who are you?'

'Ah, come on. I'm only teasing.'

'I don't like that kind of teasing,' she

said. 'Do you work at the mill?'

'No, I don't. I won't spread anything around. I was kidding.'

'You'd better be. I shouldn't really be here with you.'

Gage sighed. 'I'm sorry, Leslie. I should have realized that you're sensitive about your position in the community.'

'I'm not really sensitive.' Leslie excused her reaction to his remarks. 'I'm just cautious.'

'I understand. Really.' He smiled softly. 'Okay?'

'Okay,' she agreed, and picked up her spoon once more.

But the little incident had robbed Leslie of her conversational skills. Even if Gage had been teasing, it reminded her that she had to be careful. After all, she had no idea who she was talking to. She was spending time with a man she had only met briefly this afternoon.

She watched Gage's large tanned hands as he finished his ice cream. He had taken off his jacket and his arms were muscular beneath the black sweater. His chest looked hard as iron. He was a bit like her father in build — sure and confident in stature, except there was more vulnerability in his mouth, less steel in his eyes. Paul Fletcher's eyes had been a pale gray. Gage's were as blue as the summer sky.

'Is there a man in your life?' Gage asked suddenly.

'There are a lot of men, but no one special,' Leslie told him. 'Are there women in your life?'

'No one special. Have you ever been married?'

'No, I haven't, but I'm finding your questions rather presumptuous.'

'I'm sorry. I just wanted to clear up that situation.'

'Why? In case I was two-timing a husband tonight?' Leslie raised her eyebrows.

'No. I just sense the possibility of getting to know one another better.'

Leslie could see what was coming; it was as clear as glass. Here she was, vulnerable because of her father's death, and here he was, a self-assured sexy male, in town for a few days. He probably wanted a quick fling. Leslie was an expert at dealing with come-ons like this.

'I don't think I want to know you better, Mr. Preston,' she said.

Gage's eyes seemed to glaze over until his expression was masked. 'If that's how you feel . . . fine. Do you want more coffee?'

Leslie glanced at her watch, seeing a chance to leave. 'No, I'd better be getting home.'

'I'll walk you back,' he said, putting some money by the check. He stood up and picked up his jacket.

It was drizzling with rain now, and they kept to the side of the road, away from the beach, sheltered by the high-rise buildings that fronted English Bay.

Leslie expected Gage to leave her to return home first, but he didn't. He walked with her until she stopped outside her building, and he waited by the door while she fitted her key in the lock.

'You don't have to come any further,' Leslie told him, feeling a distinct hostility between them now. Gage hadn't taken her rejection lightly.

'I'd rather,' he said. 'Anything could happen between the elevator and your apartment.'

'But I'm used to being alone.'

'I know, but you've been with me, and I'd feel bad if anything happened to you.'

Leslie shrugged and led the way to the elevator. 'You're scaring me.'

'I'm sorry. I didn't mean to.'

'I'm quite safe here. We have security.'

Gage eyed the empty security desk. 'I noticed.'

When they were in the elevator Gage rubbed his hand across his blondish curls to shake off the moisture. Leslie watched his fingers and wondered how they would feel on her flesh. Not used to such feelings, she unzipped her jacket, very aware of his potent blue stare.

When the elevator stopped at the penthouse floor, Leslie crossed the thick gray carpet and stood with her back to her front door.

'Guarding the Fletcher treasures?' Gage asked cynically.

'I'm sorry you feel rejected,' Leslie told him, thinking that she just had to get rid of him now. 'But I don't know anything about you.'

'You will on Monday morning.'

'But in the meantime you want me to know you in another sense.'

Gage put his hands on his narrow hips. 'Did I say that?'

'Not in so many words.' Leslie wished she hadn't mentioned anything.

'I was thinking more in the light of the two of us having dinner tomorrow night, but if you'd rather not . . . ' He shrugged.

As Leslie's eyes flitted restlessly over his rough-hewn features, she realized that she didn't want to say goodbye to Gage until Monday. She needed to see him again, even if it was unwise. 'Well, if it's only dinner,' she said.

Gage put up his hands. 'I promise I won't trespass on the Fletcher property.'

Leslie knew she shouldn't really date him, but then she shouldn't have accompanied him for the ice cream. What she knew so far was that he was a good-looking, intelligent man with an elusive quality that made her pulse race. He had some business to deal with, but Monday was soon enough. Why not have some fun?

'You're persuasive,' she said huskily, still unsure.

'Then the answer's yes?' His blue eyes held hers.

Leslie nodded and produced her key from her pocket. 'Now I'd better go.'

Gage made sure she was safely inside her apartment before he left. Leslie shrugged out of her damp suede jacket and walked into the bedroom, tugging at her sweater as she went. She added her bra, jeans, socks and panties to the pile, then ran herself a hot tub. As she slid into the bubbling lavendar foam, a tingle of excitement slid through her stomach. The sensation was so elusive that Leslie treasured it. How could she deny herself a date with Gage when he made her so aware of being a woman?

★   ★   ★

With Saturday came the realization that she had no indication of what time Gage would be calling for their dinner date. Leslie hadn't even given him her unlisted phone number so he wouldn't be able to get in touch with her. Maybe he wasn't really going to take her out. Maybe the date had been a joke to get back at her for rejecting his first move, even though Gage didn't strike her as that type of man. She was sure he would follow through on his actions.

But as the day progressed her composure gradually left her. The weather didn't help. Misty fog slithered over the ocean and beach, while hardy British Columbians trudged along the seafront, indifferent to the weather.

Determined to snap out of her mood, Leslie retrieved a large atlas from her bookshelf and looked up the Canadian coast to find Preston Falls. It was a small community at the end of a long inlet, appropriately named Preston Inlet. There was also Preston Harbor and Preston River. One of the Prestons had obviously been infamous, she thought, remembering her history. He had probably been the best drinker in town.

Fletcher owned four mills in the province, the smallest being the one at Preston Falls. In keeping with her father's policy, Leslie had never visited any of the mills so she wasn't sure what she was dealing with. Gage had told her that he didn't work for Fletcher, although he could be involved with the union. But she didn't know much about the unions either. It seemed she had all the wrong knowledge. She had worked at Fletcher Paper in various capacities all through high school and college vacations, and since graduation she had been under her father's instruction full-time. She now saw this training as a good move on Paul Fletcher's part because she was ready to move into his deserted slot.

Leslie closed the atlas and rested her head on a velvet cushion. There would be someone on the board who had heard of Gage Preston. Frank might even know.

Restlessly, she looked at the digital clock on her stereo. It was past six. Should she change clothes, be ready for a date? What if she got dressed up and Gage didn't come? She had never been stood up.

She decided to take a bath, and just as she was drying herself the security phone rang. Wrapped in a green towel, Leslie ran barefoot to the living room.

'It's Gage. I'm sorry I didn't give you a definite time. I tried to get hold of your phone number, but — '

'It's unlisted,' she interrupted as the deep male voice vibrated through her body and excitement and relief made her feel as light as a feather. 'I'll let you in.'

Getting out of the towel and into underwear and a robe was all Leslie could manage by the time her doorbell rang. Not quite understanding her motives, she almost fell over herself to answer it.

Gage was wearing a pair of gray dress pants, with a white shirt and black tie beneath his black leather jacket. His hair was brushed into crisp curls, and he smelled of a subtle fresh-air aftershave that tantalized Leslie's senses.

'Good evening,' he said, his eyes roaming over the yellow silk robe.

Leslie's fingers clutched the low neckline. 'Good evening. I'm sorry I'm not dressed.'

'It's my fault. I should have asked you for your phone number. I didn't think.'

'Neither did I,' she said meekly.

He grinned suddenly, his blue eyes lighting up. 'I thought maybe you were testing me.'

'In what way?' she asked blankly.

'To see if I really meant the date. The more difficult you make it for me to get to you, the more I must want to see you if I conquer the barriers.'

Leslie smiled at his words. 'That sounds very convoluted.' She shook her head and said honestly, 'I never gave it a thought.'

He raised an eyebrow. 'Do I spot a woman without guile?'

'Possibly,' she said lightly, not wanting him to know that she was unfamiliar with many man-woman games. Then she realized that he was still standing outside her apartment door. 'Why don't you come in?'

As she closed the door, Leslie watched Gage shrug out of his jacket and throw it casually over an upright upholstered chair. She saw the ripple of muscle beneath his white shirt, and she had to stop herself from reaching out to touch him. It was such a strange response for her that she felt flustered.

'May I get you a drink?' she asked. 'I have to change, so you'll have to wait.'

'A drink sounds inviting. Scotch on the rocks if you have it.'

'Just one moment.' Leslie went to the liquor cabinet, very aware of Gage's blue eyes on her. The yellow silk clung to her figure.

She handed Gage his drink. 'Could you tell me where we're going so I'll know how to dress?'

'I thought we'd go to dinner somewhere where they have entertainment.'

'Fine. I'll just be a moment then.'

Leslie hurried into her bedroom and closed the door. Gage Preston made her act like a giddy schoolgirl. She pushed aside the mirrored closet doors with a definite shake to her hands, and stared at the line of clothes.

She chose a peach silk jumpsuit that she matched with sandals of the same color. The suit had a low zippered neckline, and she wore a gold chain at her throat. She knotted her hair, and drew down a few wisps to flutter against her cheeks. She made up sparingly. After spraying herself generously with perfume, she inhaled a breath, straightened her back and returned to the living room.

Gage was sitting on her velvet sofa, his glass of scotch cradled in his hands between his outspread knees. Their eyes met and when Gage didn't speak, Leslie allowed herself the luxury of looking at him. His broad shoulders stretched the white shirt in a manner that made her blood race, and the gray pants pulled tautly across his thighs.

As the silence remained between them, Leslie moved to the cocktail cabinet and poured herself some sherry.

Leaning against the edge of the teak cabinet, she lifted the crystal glass. 'To the evening.'

A faint smile touched the corners of Gage's mouth. 'To the evening. You sure have a nice apartment here.'

'Thank you.'

'Fit for a beautiful woman.'

'Thank you, but I've never really thought of myself that way.'

'I would have thought, being a Fletcher, that you felt it was your birthright.'

Leslie shook her head. 'My father wasn't always rich. When he was a child, he had to work to help out the family finances.'

'Did that help to make him ruthless?'

Leslie nodded. 'I suppose it did. Always having to fend for yourself to put food into your stomach. Somewhere along the way you must lose your compassion.'

Gage drained his drink and placed the glass carefully on one of her cork coasters. He stood up. 'How do you fit into the scheme?'

'What do you mean?'

'How does a compassionate daughter replace an iron-fisted father?'

'How do you know I'm compassionate?' She veiled her velvet brown eyes with long lashes.

'I'm only surmising from what I know of you. Your hard streak seems to be an act. Am I right, Les?'

His use of the short form of her name disconcerted her as much as his words. His blue eyes challenged her, but Leslie's protective coating was hard to move aside. Until she knew what Gage Preston wanted from Fletcher Paper, she couldn't trust him fully. 'That's for you to find out,' she said at last.

He smiled. 'I'll take that as an invitation.' He bent forward slightly and Leslie thought he might kiss her. Her mouth trembled, but he moved aside.

'Shall we leave?' he said.

★   ★   ★

Gage had the silver Porsche parked outside illegally.

'No ticket.' Leslie laughed as he tucked her into the front seat out of the rain, his fingers lingering on her knee.

54

Gage ducked in beside her. 'I hoped for the best because it was raining.'

'Is this your car?'

'No, it belongs to a friend, the one who also owns the apartment where I'm staying. He always goes to Hawaii for the winter.'

'He?'

'I told you I wasn't attached. I meant it.'

'Haven't you been married? I hardly ever meet men who have been single all their lives.'

'Yes, I've been married.' His words sounded rather bitter.

'What happened?'

'Oh.' Gage shrugged. 'Two stormy years and we divorced. No children, thank goodness.'

'And you've never felt the urge again?'

Gage shook his head. 'Neither have you, obviously.'

'When I was a teenager I rejected everything: the wealth, the system, marriage.'

'And now?'

Leslie glanced at him, aware of the rumble of the car, the steady ping of rain on the roof, the closed-in intimacy with this man beside her. She realized that she didn't know the answer to his question. Her father had been the influence in her life. She had spent her teenage years trying to reject him, and then made up for it by trying to please him. Now he was gone . . .

'You don't have to answer that,' Gage said softly. 'I haven't reached thirty-eight without learning how the years can speed by until we're suddenly one day made aware that there's a missing link. Your father's death has probably got you asking questions.'

'I never really had much to do with him personally,' Leslie said. 'But he was a very strong influence in my life, and it seems lonely without him.'

'It's natural, Les.'

Les, again. She stared outside as the lights streaked into red and yellow streamers on the wet road. She hadn't

talked seriously to anyone in years. Her
friends from university days had married and settled down and she had lost
touch with them. She could feel the
depth of Gage Preston's character as if
it were a living presence. She felt she
could trust him, but she had to know
more about him.

'What do you do for a living?' she
asked.

'I run a log salvaging business.'

Leslie gazed at his strong hands
encircling the black leather steering
wheel. 'Do you sell logs to Fletcher?'

'I have in the past.' He smiled
slightly. 'What I do for a living has
nothing to do with why I want to see
you. Actually, the log salvaging part of
my life is coming to a close. I'm in the
process of selling the business.'

'And then what will you do?'

'I've always wanted to write a novel.'

'How ambitious. Have you written
anything?'

'A few short stories and poems.'

'I'm impressed,' Leslie said sincerely.

'More impressive than salvaging logs.'

Her eyes twinkled. 'Oh, I'm sure log salvaging has its merits.'

'It's good to see you smile, Leslie Fletcher,' he said.

'Haven't I smiled before?'

'Not so impulsively.'

Leslie knew that Gage made her that way. He brought out her natural self and let it show. For sheer pleasure, she laughed.

Gage covered her hand with his large warm fingers. 'Keep that up and I'll fall in love with you. You're very attractive when you're happy.'

Leslie turned her hand until her palm was face up, touching his. Would he fall in love with her? What would happen then? Would she be in love with him? The thoughts made her so lightheaded that she recklessly squeezed his fingers. When Gage returned the pressure, Leslie felt the suspense heighten until she wanted to explode.

3

The restaurant was small and intimately lit, a place Leslie had been to once or twice before. Usually around ten o'clock there was dancing on the small dance floor. Gage had made a reservation, and their table was hidden behind a cascade of potted palm trees.

The menu was substantial, and Gage admitted that he had chosen the restaurant because he was hungry. Leslie was also hungry. She had been too tense all day to eat much, but now that she was actually with Gage her appetite had returned a little. She ordered a plate of Pacific shrimp and a baked potato, and left Gage to indulge himself in the largest steak.

'Tell me about the time when you rejected everything,' he asked when his hunger had been appeased somewhat.

Leslie told him about her hiking trip

across Europe with her girlfriend, Suzie, and how Suzie had eventually wound up staying in Italy to marry a man who called himself a count.

'Don't you believe that?' Gage smiled.

'Suzie tends to exaggerate, but the man is rich and they have two children, so he's real enough.'

'What happened when you came home from Europe?'

'I went to college and took the business courses my father wanted me to while I worked for Fletcher Paper.'

'How long have you been with the company full-time?'

'Five years. Maybe that's not a recommendation to run the shop, but I'm going to try hard. My father gave his entire life to the company. He might not have had such an early heart attack if he'd been able to relax more often.'

'He must have taken vacations.'

'Hardly ever. He'd combine business with any pleasure and sometimes my mother would go along as moral support.'

Gage eyed her curiously. 'You sound bitter about that.'

Leslie sighed. 'I'm not a feminist, but I do think that my mother surrendered a lot for my father. She had a promising career as a musician when she met him, but she gave it up.'

'It must have been the way she wanted it.'

'Maybe, but my father was one of those people who pressures you into doing things you don't want to do because you feel you need the praise.'

'But not you?'

'Oh, I gave in to him.'

'By working for Fletcher Paper.'

'And other ways.' Leslie suddenly felt that she was being prodded too hard. Gage's expression was very thoughtful as he questioned her. She changed the subject. 'What about your parents?'

Gage accepted the shift in the conversation. 'They live just outside of Vancouver. They were both school-teachers, now retired to tend their daffodils. A perfect life for them.'

'Why do you hide yourself in the bush?'

'I don't particularly like city life.'

His words were definite; he sounded like a man who had made up his mind and stuck to it. In the car, after his talk of love, she had gotten her hopes up, but now they drooped. Their lifestyles were so different.

'What's the matter?' Gage asked.

'Nothing,' Leslie said cheerfully. She didn't want him knowing the direction of her thoughts; they were veering up and down with her emotions. 'I looked up Preston Falls on the map. It's a long way north.'

'It's a distance,' he said, his blue eyes sharp. 'I'm surprised you didn't know about it before.'

'I knew about it, but my father had a policy that he didn't get involved with the mills on a personal level.'

'I know,' Gage said.

Leslie felt a subtle change of

atmosphere that made her feel awkward, as if she had said the wrong thing.

'Are you going to change his policies?' Gage asked.

'Maybe.' She shrugged. 'I've hardly had time to think about it.'

'I realize that.'

Leslie stared into her coffee cup with the feeling that his questions were for a very definite purpose. Whatever he wanted from her or Fletcher Paper on Monday, he was using this time to get information. She was probably being used. All his flattery and talk about love were carefully placed lures until she fell into his trap and told him everything he wanted to know. Whatever it was. She made up her mind to be more guarded.

Gage's blue eyes narrowed. 'Why so enigmatic all of a sudden?'

Leslie glanced to the dance floor where couples were dancing to a slow tune. 'Because I feel like having some fun,' she said. 'Do you dance?'

'Not usually, but if I have to, to

please you, I will.'

'Don't strain yourself,' she tossed at him.

'Les,' he chided. 'What have I done?'

Nothing yet, she thought. Except maybe raising her hopes into thinking that she might have met a man she could finally love. She stood up and held out her hand. 'Dance?'

Gage couldn't refuse her without making a scene. His hand on her waist, he moved with her to the dance floor. His arms held her lightly, but with a restrained strength Leslie knew he was capable of. She felt like burying her head against his chest and putting her arms around his waist, but instead she smiled up at him, forcing a performance she often put on for her dates.

But Gage wasn't the usual type of man she went out with. He tugged her to him, his hand sliding down the silky jumpsuit, his voice harsh in her ear. 'Don't play-act.'

With a sigh, Leslie did what she wanted to do. She rested her head lightly against him.

'That's better,' he whispered, his fingers splaying around her hip, the pressure of his thighs communicating with hers. Leslie drew in a long quivering breath. She could feel Gage's mouth in her hair.

It seemed that they were circling the dance floor forever, but it was only for two songs. When Gage took her hand to lead her back to their table she felt slightly disorientated.

'Shall we go home now?' he asked softly.

'Maybe we should,' Leslie agreed. She felt she needed some fresh air. Being with Gage was like drinking a gallon of wine.

With her honey-colored fur coat around her shoulders, Leslie walked with Gage to the car.

Settled in the low leather seat, Gage turned to Leslie. 'Is that real fur?' he asked.

'Oh, no,' she told him. 'I couldn't wear a real animal. I feel strongly about that. It's a very good fake, though.'

'I'm glad,' Gage said as he started the car.

She wondered if he were a conservationist or environmentalist, and if he were connected with an agency or something, and turned sideways in her seat to ask him.

'Let's keep business in the office,' Gage said.

'How do you know what I'm going to say?'

'Because I can easily see you putting two and two together.'

'And I'm making odd numbers,' Leslie countered. 'I don't see why you can't tell me what you want.'

Gage accelerated the car from a green light with more force than necessary. 'Why wreck the weekend?'

Leslie's throat choked up. This entire episode with Gage was a farce. Friday afternoon in the office they had said nothing. Friday evening in the ice cream parlor they had said even less. And now this date.

'Are you dating me to get me on your side?' she asked huskily.

'Leslie, forget it. It belongs in the office.'

'Then drive to the office.'

'No,' Gage said stubbornly.

Leslie watched his expression carefully, but in the dark she couldn't make out what he was feeling or thinking. 'You're playing with me,' she said tightly.

'No, I'm not.'

'Yes, you are. You have a proposal of some sort to put to me, but you're holding off, getting to know me first, hoping maybe I'll be soft toward you. Well, I won't be soft on you, Mr. Preston. I'm my father's daughter.'

'Okay.'

'What do you mean, okay?'

'Just that. You've told me what to expect and I'll work to that end.'

'And meanwhile I'm ignorant of the situation and will come into it on Monday fumbling.'

Gage stopped the car outside her building. 'You just said you were your father's daughter. I don't think your father knew what the word fumble meant.' He got out of the car and came around to Leslie's side.

Leslie stepped out on the sidewalk just as he reached to open her door.

'Independent, aren't we?'

This whole evening had developed into a slanging match. Leslie sighed. 'There's no need for you to come upstairs tonight.'

Gage ignored her words and took hold of her elbow to steer her to the glass doors. The elevator stopped three times as if someone had punched buttons and then disappeared. Luckily no one joined them as they stood on opposite sides of the doors. Leslie rushed off when they reached the penthouse suite.

'Leslie, I don't want to part on bad terms,' Gage said as he followed. 'You'll learn in time that you'll have to separate your personal life and your professional life.'

'Who are you to tell me what I'll have

to do?' Leslie asked, but she knew he was right. Her father had never been able to disassociate himself from his professional life and his family had suffered.

'I guess I'm no one. Yet,' Gage added.

His white smile melted her, but Leslie kept her expression closed; all her strict protectiveness came to the surface. 'What do you mean, yet?' she taunted.

The blue eyes roamed her face. 'Hardness doesn't suit you, Leslie.'

'Hardness is part of my nature.'

'Oh, yeah.'

Leslie didn't like his attitude toward her — he was acting as if he owned her. 'Look, Mr. Preston. I don't even know what you want from me yet. I'm hardly going to come on all sweet.'

'We'll see,' Gage said confidently, and moved forward.

Leslie was in his arms and his mouth was descending before she knew it. She couldn't fight him. She wanted to feel his mouth upon hers, taste the maleness beneath the steady pressure, rest her fingers on his shoulders and then run them down the soft leather covering his arms. She was flying, winging her way into an unknown world, a world she suddenly, desperately wanted to discover — with Gage.

When he drew away, she longed to reach out for more of his touch.

'Take care,' he said softly. 'I'll see you on Monday.'

'Monday,' Leslie repeated, dazed.

Gage punched the elevator button Just before the doors closed, he smiled. 'I had a good time tonight.'

'So did I,' Leslie whispered, and walked into her apartment. She tossed her fur coat on the sofa, and pressed her fingertips to her mouth. Her lips were still tingling, and suddenly Monday couldn't come soon enough.

★   ★   ★

Leslie had almost her entire wardrobe on the bed on Monday morning before she decided what she should wear to the office. She tried to blame her indecision on the fact that it was her first day as president and chairman of the board of Fletcher Paper, but she knew deep down she was trying to impress Gage Preston.

She had spent all day Sunday trying to figure out what he would ask her, but she was no wiser. Right now she was prepared for anything.

Finally she selected a tan wool suit. The jacket was fitted over a slim, knee-length skirt, and her blouse was ivory silk. She stepped into high-heeled tan shoes and slung a matching leather bag over her shoulder. Carrying a brown raincoat and tan briefcase, she went downstairs and slid into the gray company limousine that was waiting at the curb.

The board members were ready for her when she arrived. Coffee had been served and Frank was sitting to the left of her father's leather chair. As usual he had a pile of papers in front of him, and was busy writing.

Frank looked up when she walked through the door. 'Morning, Leslie.'

'Morning, Frank.' She glanced at the other male faces turned her way, lit by a ray of weak sunlight. 'Good morning.'

They all nodded as Leslie moved to her place. She put her briefcase on the table, but didn't take her seat. Actually, she was in awe of her father's large chair as well as the board. Trying for inward calm, she took stock of the men who faced her. Ronald Statler, in his sixties and balding, was her father's vice-president, or her vice-president now, she supposed. George Statler, his son, was in his thirties. Leslie's uncle, Ray Fletcher, was thinner than his brother, but Leslie had always found Ray more appealing and easier to get along with, even though he possessed the same hard edge of all the Fletchers. All these men had managerial positions within Fletcher Paper, as did the two younger members of the board, Alan Aranson and Peter Forbes. The old school — Finlay Dawson, Donald McIntosh and Courtland Page — were retired shareholders who only entered Fletcher Paper on Mondays for the board meeting. Leslie had been brought up with the three men, but she didn't really know them. She didn't know any of them, she thought as she slipped into her chair.

She looped her fingers in front of her, hoping she looked calmer than she felt. 'As you all sadly know, my father is no longer with us, and I'm the one left with Fletcher Paper. I haven't had a chance, obviously, to go over my father's policies, but right now, as far as I'm concerned, everything will remain the same until I look more closely at the company.' She smiled to give them all the assurance that she wasn't unsure. 'Of course,' she continued, 'you've all been at this game much longer than I, and I welcome all your suggestions and ideas as well as guidance.'

That sounded good, Leslie thought, and the board members seemed to think so too because the ideas and suggestions came fast and furious. Leslie was glad of Frank's steady presence as he recorded every word spoken.

When the meeting was over, Leslie stood at one end of the long table, while each board member shook her hand and wished her the best. She hoped they all meant it sincerely. She needed the encouragement.

By the time she went along to her office, her head was throbbing. She smiled wanly at Julie. 'Could you get me some coffee and an aspirin, please, Julie. Is Mr. Preston here yet?'

'No.' Julie shook her head. 'But here's the information you wanted on him. It was the best I could do at short notice.' She handed Leslie a file folder. 'I'll get the aspirin and coffee.'

In the office, Leslie opened the drapes, tipped all the cigarettes from the carved box into the wastebasket and put the box into the bottom drawer. She picked up the gold pen and her eyes misted as she thought of her father using it. She must have cared, only it had been hidden. His death seemed to hurt more as the days progressed and the first numbness slid away. She blinked back the tears. It was ten-thirty. She had half an hour before Gage Preston arrived.

She sat down at her desk and opened the file folder Julie had given her. Gage was age thirty-eight, and ran Preston Salvage Company, Preston Falls, British Columbia. His father was Richard Preston, a retired school-teacher. Gage had attended the University of British Columbia in Vancouver and majored in forestry with a number of impressive postgrad credits. He was known in his university years for taking active stands, especially antiwar. That's all, Julie wrote.

No more than Leslie already knew. Everything he had told her about himself had been the truth, although he had omitted the forestry degree and the antiwar stands. That aspect of him interested her.

Julie appeared at the door with coffee and aspirin.

'Thanks.' Leslie swilled down the aspirin, hoping it would stop the dull throb from progressing into a full-blown headache.

She scanned the information on Gage once more, and looked at her watch. He was due to arrive in a few minutes, and the excitement Leslie felt was overpowering.

The intercom buzzed. Composing herself, Leslie leaned forward. 'Send Mr. Preston in, Julie.'

Gage was wearing his gray suit, the jacket open to show off a pale blue shirt and navy tie. His blatant maleness disturbed Leslie in a way she wished it wouldn't.

'Good morning,' he said with a slight smile, reaching to take her offered hand.

His fingers were warm and strong. Leslie let her hand stay in his a shade too long, recalling his kiss. 'Good morning. Will you take a seat?'

Gage pulled up a leather chair. 'The weather's warmer today,' he said pleasantly.

'Yes, the weather is nice. Would you like coffee?'

'Please.'

Why bother asking? The man never refused food or drink, Leslie thought as she informed Julie of their needs.

Silence hung between them as they waited for Julie to bring in the coffee. After she had placed the tray on the desk between them, Gage laced his cup with cream and sugar, and Leslie poured herself more black coffee. She flicked a coral fingernail at the manila file in front of her. 'I've been doing some research.'

'What did you find out?'

'No more than you've already told me, except for the active stands you took at the university. Care to explain?'

Leslie thought she saw Gage tense, but it was hard to tell from his relaxed sitting position.

'Do you feel it has a bearing on what

I want of you?' he asked.

'I'm not sure, but I would like to know what you want. We've been hopping fences since we first met, and I haven't got all day.'

Gage was at once deadly serious. He put his cup on the tray and leaned forward. 'It's this, Leslie. Preston Falls is slowly being polluted by Fletcher Paper, and despite attempts during the past year to get Fletcher to initiate a cleanup, you've never paid any heed.'

'I'm not sure what you mean by Fletcher Paper polluting Preston Falls.'

'I'm talking about the waste from the mill running into the community water supply, the entire river and stream system that runs into the town.'

Leslie inhaled a breath. Whatever she had thought Gage wanted it hadn't been this, but she strived to keep cool. 'Did my father know?'

'Yes, he knew.' Gage leaned back in his chair. 'Many of the residents depend on fishing for their food supply. If something isn't done soon they will slowly be poisoned.'

Leslie fiddled with the gold pen. 'You're being dramatic, surely.'

'Have you ever seen anyone suffering from mercury poisoning?'

'No, but — '

'You wouldn't think I was being dramatic,' he interrupted. 'It causes abnormal vision, kidney disorders, impaired coordination of body movement, speech problems, swallowing difficulties and might eventually lead to a coma.'

'I see,' Leslie said slowly. 'What do you want me to do?'

'I want more pollution controls put on the mill.'

Leslie knew from a previous accounting for pollution controls on one of their mills that it was expensive. 'It costs quite a bit.'

'What's money when it comes down to human suffering?'

Leslie bit into her lower lip. 'There must have been a reason my father didn't do something.'

Gage laughed harshly. 'Surely you can figure that one out for yourself.'

'He probably didn't care,' Leslie said.

Gage smiled halfheartedly. 'I'm glad you said it.'

'How did you contact my father before?'

'The union has been to him and we've sent letters, but we never got answers.'

Leslie stared at his rugged face, full of concern for his cause. 'Are you using me as the scapegoat?'

Gage shrugged. 'I guess you could say that.'

'What if I can't do anything either?'

Gage's blue eyes grew dark. 'I have my ways of making you.'

'Oh, you do,' she challenged.

'Yes, I do, Miss Fletcher.' Gage stood up and pushed his chair aside. 'Anyhow, I'll be in town for a few more days. How about if I return on Wednesday morning to see what you have to say after you've had a think.'

'That sounds reasonable,' she told him.

He looked at her as if he wanted to say more, but he nodded instead. 'I'll see you Wednesday, Les.'

Leslie gave Gage time to leave the floor, then buzzed Julie. 'Get me Frank Lehman,' she asked.

When the dark-haired man was seated in front of her, she gave him a direct stare. 'Frank, what do you know about the Preston Falls mill?'

Frank's thin lips stretched over his even teeth; that was his smile. 'It's a steady plant. We don't make a big profit, but we don't lose. The union is quite strong, but we've only had one strike in the last three years.'

'What was the strike over?'

'Safer working conditions.'

'And did they get them?'

'We settled.'

Leslie heard the evasiveness in Frank's tone. 'What about pollution controls on the mill?'

Frank raised an eyebrow. 'We've paid some fines and put on minimal equipment.'

'Only minimal?' Leslie asked.

He shrugged. 'The cost of putting on more isn't worth the profit of the mill.'

'I guess it's cheaper to pay fines.'

'You said it,' Frank agreed.

Leslie threaded her fingers together. 'What about projected illness because of a polluted town water supply?'

Frank glanced at his carefully manicured fingernails. 'We have the mercury level checked annually, and it's not at danger level.'

'Yet,' Leslie said.

'Les.' Frank leaned forward, his hands clasped between his knees. 'There's mercury in virtually every water system these days.'

'I'm talking about Preston Falls, Frank.'

'It is getting higher in Preston Falls, I'll admit.'

'You'll admit!' She stood up and walked to the window, flicking the drapes impatiently. 'I guess these were all my father's policies.'

'He only saw dollar signs,' Frank said.

'I know.' Leslie sighed and stood with her back to the window. 'Have you heard of Gage Preston?'

'A troublemaker.'

'A troublemaker on the warpath,' Leslie clarified. 'He wants us to put pollution controls on the mill now.'

'He's been trying for a long time, Les.'

'A year, he said. Frank, get me all the documentation you can on the effects of mercury poisoning on humans. I also want information on the mill, giving me the cost of updated pollution control equipment.'

'Les, it's a fortune. You know as well as I do that the forest industry is hard-hit these days. It's not worth it for a little mill like that.'

'Frank,' Leslie warned, her voice stern. 'Do as I say.'

He stood up and put his hands on the back of the chair. 'Okay, you're the boss now. When do you need the information?'

'Wednesday morning.'

'Short-order cook, aren't you.' He smiled wryly. 'Look, I want to give you a piece of advice, Leslie. Don't let Gage Preston get to you.'

'What do you mean?'

'I mean, don't let him push you into a corner. He's using your father's death to his advantage, you realize that.'

'I know.' Leslie nodded.

'Guys like that get a little fame out of doing something like this.'

'I know all that, Frank, but I do feel that I should look into the situation.'

'Maybe you're right.' Frank looked around the office. 'Do you need any help?'

Leslie glanced helplessly at the piles of files, and especially the blank computer screen in the corner. She really didn't have a clue where to start. She did need Frank's guidance.

'I don't know anything about these things.' She pointed to the computer.

'Neither did Paul. That was his new toy. He didn't have a chance to play with it. We'll get it going.'

'In the future,' Leslie said. 'Let's get this paperwork cleared up first.'

Frank took off his jacket and rolled up his white shirt sleeves.

'They should have made you president,' Leslie said a few hours later as the hands of the clock moved past two. 'What would I do without you?'

'You'll catch on,' Frank said. 'Don't let anything worry you, and ask questions if you don't know.'

'Thank you,' she said sincerely. 'Would you mind if I get out of the office for a while? I need to clear my head.'

'Go ahead, get some lunch.'

'What about you?'

Frank picked up his black jacket. 'I have something planned.'

'Okay.' Leslie smiled. 'Thanks, again.'

The fresh spring breeze and sunshine blinking through the gray sky were what Leslie needed to pick up her spirits. She walked to a favorite restaurant, ate a sandwich and salad, and drank a glass of sparkling water.

Back in her office, she opened all the drawers to her father's desk and cleaned them out. She threw her father's pills away, and anything else she didn't think she'd need. She also dumped her photograph in the wastebasket. This was her office now.

She called Julie in. 'Could you make me an appointment with the art gallery to get some rental art?' she asked.

Julie nodded. 'Don't you like what you've got?'

'Not particularly.'

Julie's eyebrows raised. 'I see.'

Leslie didn't like the woman's attitude. There was a hint of jealousy about their positions underlying Julie's actions all the time. 'You don't see, Julie,' Leslie told her secretary firmly. 'My father was his own man. I'm my own woman. I want my own taste around me. And that includes secretaries,' Leslie added.

Julie flushed. 'I understand, Miss Fletcher. I'll call the art gallery.'

Leslie sighed as she watched the woman move to leave. 'Julie,' she called.

'Call me Leslie. We're both the same age.'

'Yes, Miss . . . Leslie.' Julie smiled slightly as she left.

Leslie felt like throwing something at the doors as they closed. Wasn't it enough that she had her father's death and her new inheritance to contend with, let alone Gage Preston and an awkward secretary?

She stopped in at the art gallery on her way home and chose half a dozen paintings to replace the ones already in her office. When she got home, she disconnected her telephone and spent an hour in a hot bubblebath. Day number one of being president of Fletcher Paper had taken its toll.

4

Frank delivered the requested information on Preston Falls Wednesday morning as promised. Leslie was astounded at the cost of putting even minimal pollution controls on the mill. She would really have to give Fletcher's financial position a thorough look before she could give any go-ahead on this project. But the effects of mercury poisoning made her sick, and she agreed with Gage that money was nothing compared to human suffering.

She left her desk to walk into the adjacent powder room. Puffing her hair with her hands, she was glad to see that the light picked out the chestnut tint this morning. Her primrose yellow silk shirt fitted her to perfection, outlining her soft breasts, and her pants were tan to match her jacket. The gold chain glittered at her throat. She was appallingly healthy and well-cared-for.

When the intercom buzzed she knew instinctively that it was Gage. She walked into the office slowly, not wanting him to think that she was eager to see him. He was in his gray suit, with a gray shirt and darker gray tie. The color scheme muted the blueness of his eyes and made them look cool.

'Good morning,' Leslie greeted him as she moved to her desk, aware of his gaze on her long legs in the well-fitting pants. 'How are you?'

His lips curved. 'I'm fine. How are you?'

Leslie smiled, her fingers pressing into the solid oak edge of the desk. 'I'm probably as fine as you are. Won't you sit down. Julie will bring coffee in.'

Gage sat down, straightening the knees of his pants as he did so. His masculinity seemed to be pronounced by whatever he wore.

Leslie took her own seat and placed her hands on the pile of documents on her desk. 'I've been studying up on

Preston Falls and pollution.'

'Good for you,' Gage said as Julie brought in the coffee tray.

Leslie noticed Julie's arm brush close to Gage's as she bent to place the tray on the desk. A sudden jealousy jolted Leslie back into her chair — an emotion she had never felt so strongly before.

Gage's blue eyes pinned Leslie down as Julie left them. 'Why so jumpy?'

'I'm not jumpy.' Leslie shrugged, trying to push down all the new sensations that were bubbling to the surface. Was she falling in love with Gage? The idea wasn't improbable, and not the first time she'd thought about it. Maybe she should think with more seriousness now. 'We're not exactly compatible business colleagues.' Leslie used the excuse of their business relationship to explain her nervousness.

'No, but at least we know where we both stand.'

'On opposite sides of the fence,' Leslie said.

'Not necessarily, Leslie. If you do something about the problem at Preston Falls, there doesn't need to be a fence.'

Leslie stood up, too restless to sit. 'Look,' she said, 'you must realize that I can't make a quick decision. I have a board to consider, and of course Fletcher's financial position.'

'I'm willing to compromise.' Gage picked up his coffee cup.

'And what if my proposal doesn't come up to your expectations?' Leslie held her breath.

Gage swilled the coffee in his cup. 'Then, with the cooperation of the union, we'll begin a number of rotating strikes at the Preston Falls mill, and escalate to other action until the Vancouver office comes to its senses.'

'But that's blackmail.'

'It sounds that way, yes,' he agreed.

Leslie crossed her fingers behind her back. 'Will you hold off with any militant action until I've done an investigation?'

'I'm not unreasonable. If you're ready to negotiate, then I'm willing to bide my time.'

'Will you wait until I've written a proposal and presented it to my board for a decision?'

Gage nodded. 'Okay.'

Relief flooded Leslie that he had given her more time.

'Maybe it would also be wise for you to visit Preston Falls,' Gage suggested.

'That would be a good idea. I'll arrange something later.'

'Sounds good to me.' Gage put down his cup, and glanced at his gold watch. 'It's a little early, but would you like to have lunch with me?'

Leslie wasn't really hungry, but she wanted to be with Gage. It was a primitive urge, something she couldn't seem to control. She had the feeling that if she declined, he would go outside and ask Julie in her place. 'Sounds good to me.' Leslie repeated Gage's words.

★   ★   ★

A sunny breezy day greeted them as they stepped through the swinging glass doors of the Fletcher Tower. Gage held Leslie's arm. 'We'll get some sandwiches and sit and watch the boats.'

Leslie couldn't think of anything more pleasant. They purchased salmon sandwiches and canned soda before walking to a plaza, where they sat down on a concrete seat surrounded by cedar shrubs and beds of purple and yellow crocuses.

Gage put their lunch down beside him. He took Leslie's hand and rubbed it between his large ones. 'Les, the other night in the ice cream parlor.'

'Yes.' She glanced at him, shivers of anticipation running through her.

'Did you really mean that about not wanting to get to know me better?'

'Well.' Leslie's cheeks grew warm despite the cool ocean breeze. 'I wasn't sure what you wanted.'

'I know.' He squeezed her hand. 'Les, at first maybe I did intend to go after you because of who you were, but not

93

after I'd met you.'

'Am I that unappealing?'

He grinned and lifted her fingers to his mouth. 'Just the opposite. You're too appealing.'

Leslie's breath caught in her throat. 'Is there something wrong with that?' she asked jerkily.

'I don't want to hurt you.'

'Are you going to hurt me?' She tried to read the answer to her question in his features, but his eyes were more confused than anything.

'I could, couldn't I? If things didn't work out.'

'Let's hope they do,' she said breathlessly, and closed her eyes briefly as his lips caressed her hand. When he let go, her fingers felt cold.

'Let's get to the food,' Gage said huskily. 'I have a rule. I never kiss a woman on an empty stomach.'

'Are you going to kiss me?'

Gage held the package containing their lunch in midair. 'Do you want me to kiss you?'

'Very much,' she said softly.

His eyes darkened until they were almost black. 'After lunch,' he promised. 'For dessert.'

Leslie laughed to break the tension as she took her sandwich from him. 'We're supposed to be watching the boats.'

'I'd rather watch you. Your hair is the color of chestnuts, your eyes like chocolate ice cream and when you laugh your voice sounds like a tinkling waterfall.'

'Eat your lunch,' Leslie scolded. 'All you think about is food.'

'Food and kissing you,' he teased, his wink and provocative conversation making Leslie's cheeks flush.

Gage laughed. 'And you blush so perfectly.'

'You'll probably use it to your advantage.'

'Probably.'

'For someone who doesn't like being teased himself, you can sure hand it out.'

'How do you know I don't like being teased?'

'You didn't like it on Friday when I called you a true, blue British Columbian.'

'Was that teasing?'

Leslie stared at him. 'Of course it was teasing.'

'There's a difference between teasing and being put down. You, Miss Fletcher, know how to put someone down.'

Leslie knew what he meant, and it was a failing that had come from continuously having to defend herself to her father. 'An inherited trait, no doubt,' she said lightly.

Gage swallowed some soda from the can. 'You think you're like your father, but from what I've heard, he really didn't care. He walked over people who couldn't help his career, and used the ones who could. You aren't like that, Les.' Gage moved along the concrete seat until his thigh was alongside hers. 'You're a beautiful woman. You do things to me that another woman hasn't done for years.'

'What things?' Leslie asked innocently.

'Birds and bees things,' he murmured and kissed the tip of her nose. 'Tell me that I do the same things to you.'

'I don't know,' she said honestly.

'Do I leave you cold?'

'No.' She shook her head, her hair glimmering in the sunshine. She felt embarrassed. She couldn't tell him that she'd reached twenty-eight without experiencing love. 'I just don't think we should get involved.' She covered her hesitation by using her usual way out. Only this time it seemed harder to do.

'Give me one good reason why not?'

'We're in competition with one another.'

'We don't need to be. If your proposal is passed by the board, then we won't be involved on a business basis anymore.'

'And what if it's not passed?' Leslie pleated the material of her tanned slacks as an icy finger slipped along her spine.

'Let's cross that bridge when we come to it, Les. Why put hypothetical obstacles in the way?'

They were concealed from prying eyes by a concrete pillar, and Leslie knew, as Gage's head lowered, that he was going to kiss her. She wanted it so much that she parted her lips provocatively.

He raised an eyebrow, but didn't comment. The mouth that covered hers was cool from the salty breeze, very male and firm. Leslie's lips trembled beneath his as shivers cascaded through her. A man's kiss had never made her want to respond so much before. She had never felt the need to reach up, as she was doing, to stroke his hair, her fingers entwining in the curls, finding them soft and not as crisp as she had expected.

She let out a little gasp of pleasure and thrust her hands more firmly into his hair.

'That feels so good,' Gage told her, his mouth raining kisses over her face.

Then he was kissing her lips again, his hands holding her arms against her sides, his fingers a hard pressure as if they really wanted to be roaming her body but the place was far too public.

His breath uneven, Gage drew away and left a few inches between them on the bench.

'I'm in town until tomorrow morning,' he said thickly.

Leslie knew what her response should be if she were sophisticated. She would invite him to her apartment and make love with him. She balled up her sandwich wrapping nervously.

'Do you feel that I'm a class beneath you?' Gage asked suddenly.

Leslie was surprised by his question. 'No, of course not.'

'I've had that impression a couple of times.'

She remembered her reaction to the ice cream parlor and she colored. He wasn't the usual type of man she dated. He was sexier, almost raw in his appeal to her.

Gage grimaced. 'I thought so.'

Leslie touched his arm, her fingers pressing into the silvery gray suit material. She stroked upward, longing for him. 'You're just different.'

'Different because I can make you react to me?'

Leslie bit into her lower lip. 'Partly.'

'We could have a lot of passion, Leslie.' His next kiss was hard and desperate.

When Leslie drew away her breath was coming in gulps. She felt the passion he talked about, rising, threatening to overtake her. But it was all so new it scared her. She stood up and tossed the wrappings and empty soda can in the litter bin.

He grabbed her arm, standing up himself. 'Don't run away from me.'

Leslie almost melted into his body, but managed to keep herself upright. 'I should get back to work, Gage.'

'Okay, I'll let you. How about if we go to a movie together?'

'A movie?' Leslie couldn't help smiling.

'I don't get to see many movies, and I really want to see you tonight.'

'And you think a movie is all I'll go for?' Leslie asked.

'I think it's all I should go for as well,' he said softly. 'You're probably right about not getting too involved.'

So now he was backing off. Maybe her kisses didn't turn him on the way he had thought they might. But the pull toward this man was like a magnet that wouldn't let go.

'What time will you pick me up?' she asked.

His smile was also relief. 'I'll come for the early show. We'll have something to eat afterward.'

'Okay,' she agreed.

'I'll see you at six-thirty,' Gage confirmed.

'Fine. 'Bye, thanks for lunch.'

''Bye, Les.' He squeezed her arm and let go.

Leslie could feel him watching her as she walked across the plaza and down the steps. When she knew she was out of his view, she exhaled a long shaky breath and walked rapidly to the office.

Upstairs, she went directly to the powder room and gazed in the mirror at her glistening eyes and flushed cheeks. She touched her mouth with her fingertips, recalling Gage's kisses. He wanted passion between them. Could Leslie give him that? She always thought she was cold toward men, but now her veins were burning with heat. Right now she wanted Gage Preston.

She pressed her hand to the cool white tile. There were other problems as well. If she gave into him, she could be making herself vulnerable to his demands over Fletcher Paper. There was so much he didn't know about her, and when he found out he could use the discovery to his advantage. Not that she really felt he was that type of man, but he had admitted, only this lunch break, that he'd come to Vancouver planning to seduce her until he'd met her. If that wasn't ruthless, even arrogant, she didn't know what was. Maybe she was putting him on a pedestal and he didn't deserve the honor. Maybe, deep down, he was just like her father. He would take her love and toss it aside when he had her where he wanted her.

She punched the tile with her fist, tears of frustration brimming from her eyes. Why was the one man who attracted her after so many lonely years possibly her enemy? She felt cheated.

★   ★   ★

Excitement about her date with Gage won out over Leslie's conflicting emotions. She rushed home at six, quickly showered and dressed in a pair of dark green tailored slacks and a leaf green silk blouse with ruffled sleeves and neckline. When Gage rang her bell, she was putting the finishing touches to her hair and makeup.

'Gorgeous as usual, Miss Fletcher,'

he said as she let him in.

Leslie's eyes flew over him, realizing that seeing him was now becoming a necessity to her. His charcoal gray slacks, white shirt and leather jacket made his hair, slightly damp as if he'd had a recent shower, look crisp and vital. Leslie imagined him getting ready to come to see her, and wondered if his thrill matched her own.

'Your eyes are shining,' Gage told her, bending to kiss her as if he couldn't help the action. 'Tell me it's for me.'

'Maybe,' Leslie said coyly, not wanting to admit to the churning sensations inside. She wasn't definitely sure what was happening right now.

She certainly couldn't think straight with Gage so near. As his mouth brushed hers and she tasted his maleness combined with the slight tang of toothpaste, she melted into his arms. She wanted the thrust of his hard thighs, the stroke of his hands down her back, over her hips, but when his fingertips brushed her breasts, she tensed.

'Not a lady to be rushed,' Gage whispered, withdrawing his lips gently. He dropped his arms. 'Are you ready?'

'Yes.' Leslie picked up a tan leather bomber jacket and Gage helped her on with it.

The movie was funny and sad, a love story. Leslie found herself identifying with the heroine. Was the woman experiencing the same feelings with the hero as she was with Gage? Did her heart tug when she looked at her man? Did her senses spring to life? Did she long to be kissed, hugged, held in his arms?

After the movie they went to a restaurant in Chinatown where they ordered a mixture of shrimp, vegetables and rice to accompany their pot of Chinese tea. Gage wanted to discuss the movie. 'What did you think?' he asked.

'I really enjoyed it,' Leslie said enthusiastically.

'It was touching,' Gage agreed. 'But kind of defeating in the end. The woman surrendered to the hero.'

'What's wrong with that? She loved him.' Then Leslie realized what she had said. She had always accused her mother of being soft and using love as an excuse to give in to her father. But right now if Gage said the word, and if — that big if — they didn't have a conflict of business interests, she would probably have a relationship with him.

Her definite decision startled her. Was she in love with him, or was it just physical attraction? When he looked at her with his warm blue gaze she felt weak at the knees and her heart thumped unsteadily.

'Then you believe in love?'

'I don't know,' Leslie said truthfully.

'Haven't you ever been in love?' Gage asked with a lift of his eyebrows.

She shook her head. 'I don't think so.'

He looked puzzled. 'Then all your affairs have been purely physical?'

All her affairs! Leslie almost laughed, but she had already told him more about herself than anyone else knew. She couldn't reveal the fact that she was untouched. Not only would he probably drop her like a hot potato but, as she'd thought before, it might put her at a definite disadvantage in the business arena. Gage would likely figure that someone inexperienced at love would also be inexperienced at work.

So Leslie evaded his direct question. 'I haven't had time for the complications of love.'

She could see that Gage didn't like her answer, and she could quite understand why. It made her seem hard, out for what she could get, like her father. But she couldn't tell him the truth.

His next words confirmed her suspicions. 'A true Fletcher.'

'I guess I am,' she agreed, knowing that she had probably lost him — unless he wanted one of her purported affairs. But suddenly love seemed very important.

Gage got to his feet. 'Let's go,' he said abruptly.

Gage drove her home in his friend's Porsche, parked it by the side of the road outside her apartment with his usual disregard for road signs and went up the elevator with her.

Outside her penthouse door, Gage thrust his hands irritably in his pockets. 'If you weren't wealthy to start with, I'd wonder who had paid for all this,' he said roughly.

Leslie shook her head as his words penetrated. She had got herself into a tangled web with her protective untruth.

'Nothing to say?' he barked. 'I know I'm not perfect, and what I told you at lunch must make me look rotten, but the women I have taken to bed have been true lovers. I wouldn't want to be used.'

'What would I have been?' Leslie asked, suddenly firing into anger.

'A business merger,' he said harshly, and walked to the fire door. 'How many floors down?'

'A lot,' Leslie said cantankerously.

'I need to let off steam,' Gage said. 'Goodnight. I'll be in touch.'

Leslie stared as the fire door slammed shut. It took her a few minutes before she found her key. She flung her jacket, purse and keys on her sofa, and ran to the window. She didn't feel that Gage had really gone until she saw the Porsche draw away from the curb on the street below.

5

Leslie buried herself in the financial details on Fletcher Paper at Preston Falls, hoping it would get her mind off Gage, but it seemed to have the opposite effect. Each time she saw the word Preston, she would drift into a dream world. Why, of all the men in the world, did I have to fall for him? she asked herself over and over again.

But his appearance had made her see how barren her life was. She was desperately lonely, and even when she tried to blame her volatile feelings on spring, on the arrival of the sun after a long rainy winter, she couldn't get Gage out of her mind. Just thinking about him sent her pulse racing.

As she delved into her report for the board, she knew she would have to visit Preston Falls before she was able to present a full picture. That meant contact with Gage again.

Julie buzzed her intercom. 'Yes,' Leslie said impatiently. The lists of figures were making her head spin.

'Leslie, Gage Preston is here to see you.'

Leslie's throat constricted. 'Just the man I want to see,' she said huskily. 'Send him in.'

Leslie stood up, smoothing her caramel silk dress. On high heels, the same shade as her dress, she walked around the desk to greet Gage.

It was the first time he'd ever worn his tight blue jeans to the office. His concession to business was in his blue shirt and navy tie. He was carrying his black leather jacket.

His lips twitched with amusement. 'I see you're now, *Leslie Fletcher, President*, in real gold.'

Leslie nodded. 'Quite impressive, don't you think?' He seemed to have forgotten their hostile parting last week.

'Very impressive. It really makes you a true, blue British Columbian.'

Leslie laughed, remembering their first encounter.

Gage put his jacket carefully over the back of a chair, then stuffed his hands in his back pockets. 'Les, forgive me for last week.'

The last thing Leslie had expected was an apology. After all, he was the victim of her prevarication. But to tell him the full truth would be to lay her soul bare.

'We were both overwrought,' she admitted, which was half the truth.

He shook his head. 'When I look back on it, and think about what I was planning to do with you . . . and then I came on all self-righteous. Your love affairs are really none of my business.'

'Well, that's true,' she agreed.

'Forgiven?' Gage stretched out his hand.

'Forgiven,' Leslie said as her fingers melted into the heat of his.

Gage let his hand drop. 'I didn't only come for the apology, although it was weighing on my mind. We still have outstanding business. Have you been to your board yet?'

'No,' Leslie said. 'I think I should visit Preston Falls first.'

'Fine with me,' he told her and took a seat, stretching out his long legs in a weary gesture.

For the first time since he came into the office, Leslie noticed the lines of strain digging into his tanned cheeks. Immediately her heart throbbed, but it was a different feeling from the passion of their previous meetings. She wanted to reach out and soothe away his tiredness. Legs trembling, she almost fell into her chair.

Gage's blue eyes assessed her. 'That's a very pretty dress.'

He was full of surprises today. 'Thank you,' she said, politely accepting the compliment.

He grinned. 'You really are something when you put on the Fletcher snobbery.'

'I'm not a snob,' she retorted, wanting to rid him of that opinion.

'Yes, you are. Your nose twitches.'

Gage chuckled. 'I'm looking forward to your visit to Preston Falls.'

'Why?' Leslie asked curiously.

'Because you'll think it's a real one-horse logging town, and probably, like your father, will wonder what all the fuss is about.'

'Let's hope I can be more objective,' Leslie told him.

'Let's hope so,' he agreed. 'Do you want me to fly you up?'

'Don't tell me you have a plane?' she said sarcastically, a little nonplussed that he would find her so humorous.

'With two wings and an engine, Les.'

'And a pilot?'

'I fly it myself.'

'My, aren't we cool.'

'You'll be glad I am if the plane gets into difficulty,' Gage remarked. 'Do you want to go up tomorrow?'

Leslie nodded. 'It's short notice, but I'm sure I can make arrangements.'

'Then I'll pick you up by cab in the morning.' Gage stood up and shrugged into his jacket.

'We can have a limousine take us to the airport. I'll have the driver collect you after he's come for me. Do you want to leave me your address?'

Gage came around her desk, reached for the gold pen and a pad and wrote down a Westend Vancouver address and telephone number.

His nearness pressed Leslie into her desk so she could hardly breathe. She could smell his foresty aftershave and the leather scent of his jacket. She felt like tugging on the edge to get his attention, but she controlled her fingers.

'That's my friend's place,' Gage said softly, close to her ear. 'It'll be interesting to arrive at the airport in a limo. I forgot I was dealing with the elite.'

'Don't keep reminding me,' she snapped. 'And don't fool yourself, Mr. Preston. You have friends who spend the winter months in Hawaii, who own Porsches, and you have your own plane. Don't call me the elite.'

Gage grinned and moved away to

leave. 'Next time I see you I'll think up an answer to that one, Miss Fletcher. Until tomorrow.'

Leslie felt like flinging the crystal paperweight at him, but she stopped herself. She picked up the piece of paper to study his heavy writing and she tucked the note into her purse. She would probably be away a couple of days and needed to alert the management at the mill at Preston Falls of her arrival, and she had to pack. She would also have to find a place to stay, although she didn't mind a local motel for a couple of nights. She'd cross that bridge when she arrived in the Falls. She would also have to tell her mother that she would be away.

★ ★ ★

Caroline Fletcher lived in West Vancouver overlooking the entire city. As Leslie wound her metallic brown BMW up the incline to the house, the sun was shining and glinting on the roofs of the downtown high-rises. She could always spot the Fletcher Tower because the top of the building peaked into a white concrete pyramid.

The ocean surrounding the city looked blue in the clear marine air, and the scent of pines and cedars reached her nostrils as she stopped her car in the driveway.

Leslie had never particularly liked the home that her parents had moved into when she'd been ten. She found the wide stone steps leading to the double oak front door pretentious, and she hated large white marble pillars. The latticed bay windows were draped and silent as she rang the doorbell.

Her mother's housekeeper, Betty Randall, answered the door. 'How are you, Les?' she asked in her down-to-earth British accent. 'Your mum's expecting you.'

'Thank you.' Leslie smiled at the tall gray-haired lady who had been with the Fletchers since Leslie's birth. 'How is she?'

'Very sad, obviously, but holding her own. We all miss your dad even though he wasn't at home very much.'

'I know,' Leslie told her.

'I'll get you some tea.' Betty rushed off, her low-heeled shoes making no sound on the thick apple green rugs that ran through the entire house.

Leslie fingered the strap of her tan purse and gazed around. Somehow this large, square foyer had never seemed like home. The only thing she'd ever had the desire to do with the winding staircase was slide down the solid oak banisters. She'd never dared. Her father's presence had forever loomed.

'Is that you, Leslie?' Her mother's voice came from the living room.

'Yes, I'm just coming in, Mother.' Leslie straightened her shoulders and walked through the door.

French windows opened to a long green lawn where yellow crocuses and pure white snowdrops reared through the winter leaves. Meandering pathways and small arbutus trees added to the natural landscape, while a swimming pool lay dormant amongst gray patio stones and redwood dressing rooms.

Caroline Fletcher lounged on an evergreen velvet sofa, her head resting on a paler, leaf green cushion. A silky gray rug covered her legs and most of her black silk dress.

'I was just getting some air.' Caroline smiled at her daughter. 'It's such a beautiful day.'

'Have you been for a walk?' Leslie bent to kiss her mother.

'Oh, I had a little scoot around. I feel very tired, Les. Betty suggested that I have a few people over on Saturday night to cheer me up, and I agree. You will come?'

'Of course,' Leslie told her, reminding herself to be home from Preston Falls by then. She sat in a green velvet armchair and let her purse sink into the thick rug.

'Tired, darling?' Caroline asked.

'I've been thrown in oars first,' Leslie said wryly.

'That bad, huh? I don't know if it was very wise of your father to leave you with such responsibility. I think a man — '

'I'm quite capable,' Leslie interrupted. 'I just have a lot of work.' She turned to smile at Betty, who put down a small round tray with tea and sandwiches.

'Make sure your mother eats something,' Betty told Leslie as if Caroline weren't in the room.

Caroline made a face at Betty's scurrying back. 'She does fuss.'

'Probably not without reason. The sandwiches look delicious. I'll pour the tea.' Leslie poured two full cups and picked up a handful of the small sandwiches.

'You don't visit me enough, Les.' Caroline took a sandwich as if she were being forced.

'I come as often as I can.' Leslie sighed.

'If you told me your time was being taken up by a man instead of work, I wouldn't mind.' Caroline smiled. 'I've given up all hope of grandchildren.'

'Mother, let's not get into that,' Leslie protested. That type of comment had started more than one argument over the past few years. 'What would you say if I told you that I had been seeing a man?' Leslie added casually.

'I would be delighted and shocked. Are you telling the truth?'

'Absolutely. I'm flying up to Preston Falls with him tomorrow morning.'

'And where's Preston Falls?'

'We have a paper mill there.'

'Like your father, you combine business with pleasure.' Caroline sighed and reached for a second sandwich. 'These are good, aren't they. Who is he?'

Leslie smiled. 'His name is Gage Preston, and yes, it is business, but . . .'

'You more than just like him,' Caroline said perceptively.

Leslie nodded, thankful to have told someone about her feelings for Gage.

'Well, I think that's the first time you've ever told me that, Les. I hope it works out for you.'

'A husband comes before grandchildren,' Leslie commented.

'Let it take its course. Sometimes these things need time to develop.'

'Was it like that with Dad?'

Caroline's eyes misted over. 'Oh, yes. Paul was my knight in shining armor. The only man I ever loved.'

'Were you the only woman he ever loved?'

'Les.' Caroline leaned forward. 'Your father might have been a lot of things. I don't hold him up for inspection as a saint, but he was never promiscuous with other women. He was a one-woman man.'

'How did you know you were in love?'

'I wanted to be with him night and day.'

'And what about him?'

'He wasn't quite as rich when I met him. My family was very well off. He didn't want me to think he was after my money, so he was quite cool for a long time, but eventually we couldn't stay away from each other.'

'That doesn't sound like Dad,' Leslie said.

'People change. As he got more and more powerful, he became money hungry and a bit of a workaholic, but I still loved him. It doesn't stop, Les. So what's this man look like? Is he handsome?'

'Very.' Leslie smiled. 'Like Dad, a bit.'

Caroline nodded. 'I knew you'd have to find a man like your father. They're rare.'

'I know.' Leslie put down her teacup.

'If it's love, Leslie,' her mother said, 'don't let it slip away.'

'I'll try not to,' Leslie said, but she wasn't sure. Even though Gage had forgiven her, she had lied to him about her love life. And then there were all the problems related to the pollution at Preston Falls and Fletcher Paper. Even if she could surmount the personal ones, she might not be able to conquer the business side.

Gage pushed his black leather bag onto the back seat of the limousine beside Leslie the next morning. He stretched out his long denim-clad legs and smiled. 'So, how are you?'

'I'm fine.' She looked with amusement at the bag beside her. 'Afraid I might leap across the seat at you?'

Gage laughed. 'You never know, but I was thinking more of stopping myself from leaping across at you.'

Leslie's fingers nervously fiddled with the turtleneck of her ribbed brown wool sweater.

Gage watched the gesture, his glance sweeping her tailored brown pants and tan leather boots, softly expensive like her jacket. 'Would you like me to leap on you, Les?'

Leslie moistened her lips, her eyes unconsciously traveling the breadth of his wide chest covered by his black wool sweater. She wondered how they had gotten into a verbal sparring match so soon in the day. 'That's a leading question.'

'Then give me a leading answer.'

His voice was husky, his eyes as blue as the sky outside. Leslie stared out the window as the suburban houses of Vancouver slipped by. 'I think we should stick to business,' she said.

Gage settled himself into the corner of the leather seat, putting his bag between his booted feet. 'And that's the final word?'

'Don't you think it's wise?' she asked.

'Oh, Les.' He sighed.

Leslie opened her mouth to tell him the truth about herself, but his blue stare was strangely vacant.

Gage looked around the limousine. 'This is pretty nice, eh? It's like gliding along in a vacuum.'

Leslie heard a raspy edge to his deep voice. 'Is that an insult?'

'Did it sound like an insult?'

'Yes.'

'Then it probably was an insult.'

'Against me personally, or against my

lifestyle?' Leslie demanded, remembering that he already thought she was a snob.

'Probably against you because rejection has never been a fun thing for me.'

'Don't tell me about rejection,' she said.

Gage looked interested. 'Then you tell me.'

He had her captured. She had nowhere to turn as he moved closer to her, his thigh nudging hers. 'Tell me, Les.'

'It's nothing to do with you.'

'It's everything to do with me.' He took her hand. 'You've been coming on to me with your eyes since the day we met in the cemetery.'

'What a romantic place to meet!' Leslie tried to drag her hand away because his touch was so disturbing, but he held her firmly.

'We had to meet somewhere, and where more appropriate than the place where you buried the man you tried so hard to love.'

Leslie choked, staring down at their linked hands. He wasn't holding her so hard now, and his fingers were soothing.

'Was he the man who rejected you, Les?'

She shook her head desperately.

'Don't deny it,' Gage said quietly. 'I won't hold it against you.'

'I don't like you,' Leslie said. Gage was touching parts of her psyche that she had never exposed to anyone else.

'Yes, you do. You just don't like the truth.'

'I'm aware of the truth, but my relationship with my father has nothing to do with you.'

'I think you're wrong, Les. Your relationship with your father is the very factor that tells me how to relate to you.'

'Who do you think you are?'

'Les.' Gage sighed.

'And don't call me Les. It's reserved for my family and friends.'

Gage grinned. 'You're quite a little spitfire, aren't you. I can see why your father felt he was leaving the company in capable hands. You won't take any . . . nonsense.'

He had been about to say a cruder word, and Leslie's lips twitched unwillingly. Every encounter she had with Gage was uncontrolled. Each moment presented a different emotion.

'Scared of being the tough bushman with me, Mr. Preston?' she asked silkily. 'You can swear. I can take it.'

'I prefer not to swear in front of ladies. It's my puritan upbringing.'

'Don't give me that,' she scorned. 'I bet you haven't got a puritanical bone in your body.'

'I'm sure there must be one. If you want to find out, just give me the word, and I'll turn off the business side of me.'

'Your line won't work on me,' she told him. The man infuriated her. Leslie felt as if she were being battered through a blender.

'I thought it was romantic.' Gage went into a mock huff.

'I couldn't imagine you being romantic. You're obnoxious.'

Gage's fingers tightened around hers. 'Come on, Les. Remember who you're slinging insults at. I can destroy Fletcher Paper if I have to.'

'You wouldn't dare,' she gritted, but she knew he would dare.

He made sure she was holding his stare while his body loomed close to hers. 'You might think I'm an ignorant uneducated bushman, but you're wrong. Log salvaging is a profitable business. I've got enough cash stashed away to go through with a fight if I have to.'

'Are you waging war?' Leslie asked tautly, a little scared of what the future might hold. Not only in her private life, but also in her business life.

Gage dropped her hand as if it had suddenly turned burning hot. 'Only if you want war.'

Leslie flexed her fingers on her knee, feeling emotionally crushed. But she was going to have to snap out of that mood. Gage Preston was a stubborn man. As president of Fletcher Paper she was going to have to stop his threats, or at least cool him down until she had scouted the situation with her own eyes.

She smiled, a beguiling smile that belied her strong words. 'Cold war for the time being, Mr. Preston.'

6

Gage's plane was small and intimate. Leslie had to share the cockpit with him, which wasn't to her liking. She would have preferred to sit and watch his back.

'You can always sit on the floor,' Gage said, sensing her mood, 'but it might be a trifle uncomfortable.'

'I'm fine,' she told him, fastening her seat belt. 'Are you sure you know how to fly this thing?'

He grinned. 'I took a few lessons last week. Now hang on, we're going up.'

He was a good pilot. Leslie had never been frightened of flying and had often flown in small planes. She amused herself by gazing downward, following the pattern of green pine-studded islands washed by blue rivers of ocean. Mountains, concealed behind a veil of mist, drifted beneath them.

Gage spoke for the first time as the plane lost altitude. 'That's Preston Inlet,' he said, pointing out a ribbon of blue. 'The town is on the inlet a few miles inland.'

'What about the river?' Leslie asked.

'That runs out of the inlet and winds through town. We'll go over it when we land.'

He was right. The landing strip at Preston Falls was so short that one minute they seemed to be dropping toward the river and the next they were on the ground.

To cover the slight rush of nervousness she had felt, Leslie joked. 'I thought you said *over* the river, not *in* it.'

Gage laughed. 'I'm sorry about that. I should have warned you.'

'I'll survive.' Leslie stood up to leave the plane.

A young, dark-haired man greeted them as Gage helped Leslie down the steps.

'This is Donny Craig,' Gage introduced the man. 'Leslie Fletcher, Don.

Don's the mechanic out here at the airport.'

Don only showed mild surprise at her name by lifting one dark eyebrow. 'Pleased to meet you.' He smiled, shaking hands with Leslie.

'Me too,' Leslie said, and then Gage and Don were moving forward.

She followed, looking around at the small hut which she supposed served as an airport office and waiting room. There were two gray hangars, and a number of small planes surrounding them. The background was the ever-present forest. Leslie sniffed the scent of pine and the sulfury smell of the mill, and her ears picked up a muffled roar.

She caught up with Gage, forgetting that they had been cloaked in hostility during most of the flight. 'What's that roar?'

'That's the falls,' Gage said. 'You'll get used to it after a while and forget it's there.' He pointed in the direction of a brown truck. 'That's my truck'

— he handed Leslie a set of keys — 'go wait, and I'll finish up here and bring our luggage.'

The keys were warm from Gage's pocket, leaving a pool of heat in her palm. Trying not to let him bother her, Leslie walked briskly away, her boots crunching on the sandy gravel. When she reached the pickup, she unlocked both doors and climbed in the passenger side.

Through the windshield which was smeared with insects and mud, she saw Gage leave the terminal to trot back to the plane. He reappeared with their luggage and joined her at the truck, tossing the bags in behind the seats. 'All set?' he asked Leslie.

'It's certainly the bush,' she remarked.

'It certainly is,' he agreed, amused. 'Where are you going to stay?'

'The local hotel or motel,' she said. 'I'm not fussy.'

Gage didn't say anything, but started the engine and bumped over the road. There was a hill down into town. If you could call it a town, Leslie thought, eyeing the hotel with the wooden veranda that gave it a Wild West flavor. A man stumbled from the front door, and she turned away.

'I don't think I want to stay there,' she said, glancing at the other buildings on the street. There was a supermarket, a general store, a bank, a liquor store and a restaurant, all leading down to Preston Harbor. The dock was moored with fishing vessels and barges between the log booms. On the opposite side, in a secluded cove, was a marina filled with shiny sailboats. Large houses crawled up a tree-split rock face. Leslie noticed a modern café with a green awning, and a motel sign.

She pointed to the sign. 'Maybe there.'

Gage drove alongside the marina and stopped outside the motel. Leslie looked at the tumbledown wooden cabins and overgrown courtyard. There was someone sitting inside the office, reading a newspaper.

Gage said quietly. 'Les, you can only get to Preston Falls by air or sea. If you live here you either own your own transportation, or charter vessels to get out. It's not a tourist town.'

'You mean this is the only motel?'

'That's what I mean.' Gage sighed. 'I thought maybe you would have arranged to stay with someone from Fletcher.'

'I don't know anyone well enough,' Leslie said, wondering what she was going to do.

'Well, I've got a spare bedroom in my cottage. It's comfortable because my family often comes and stays with me. You're welcome.'

Leslie turned to look at him, and found his blue expression completely open and honest.

He shrugged. 'Strictly business.'

'It would be better than this place.' Leslie indicated the cabins.

'Well, it's not the Ritz, but it's comfortable and clean.' Gage laughed. 'But I don't want you twitching your nose at it. I built the house myself and

I'm proud of it.'

'I don't twitch my nose,' Leslie protested.

'Yes, you do.' Gage started the engine again, and bumped off along the road. 'When are you going to the mill?'

'I wasn't sure what time we would arrive today, so I made an appointment with Cliff Daniels first thing tomorrow morning.'

'That's fine.' Gage stopped the truck on a mound overlooking the town.

From this direction Leslie could see the frothy white falls, the roar even more apparent. To one side of the river and falls was the Fletcher Paper mill. The letters FP were painted in white down one side of the tall chimney-stacks.

'That's your baby,' Gage said.

'It looks interesting,' Leslie told him as she looked at all her father had worked so hard for. She felt a sudden elusive tie to the mill.

'Look up beyond the mill,' Gage suggested.

Leslie glanced up the hillside. 'What am I supposed to be looking at?'

'All those bare slopes,' he said wryly. 'They look like they've been raped.'

Gage turned in his seat, his arm hung over the steering wheel. 'An appropriate description. They should have been reforested years ago. Instead, there's minor growth, but it won't be a forest again in our lifetime.'

Leslie shook her head. 'You can't blame that on my father. There are loads of logging operations in the area.'

'Granted. I'm not accusing him of every crime in the book. I'm just pointing out how industry destroys the environment.'

Leslie didn't answer his comment because she didn't know what to say that wouldn't sound as if she were taking sides. She had to evaluate the situation at Preston Falls carefully on her return to Vancouver before she made her presentation to the board.

Gage turned the key to the engine. 'Now I'll show you my home.'

Leslie genuinely loved Gage's log house. He'd hand-built the wooden veranda and the log chairs. Inside, a large brick fireplace centered the cottage to add extra heat in the winter months. A typewriter stood on a small oak desk, while books lined the rough-hewn wooden shelves. The kitchen was fitted with modern accessories, the operation made possible by a generator hooked up from a small stream that passed the back of the property. Sofa, chairs and beds were all handmade, Gage explained as he showed Leslie into the spare bedroom and tossed her suitcase on the bed.

Leslie liked his color scheme of thick rust carpet and dusky orange drapes and comforter, and told him so.

'It's me,' he said with a trace of pride.

'It's fine, Gage.' The curtains were fluttering in a soft breeze over a brown velour armchair and an oak dresser with a mirror.

Leslie turned to him. 'I love it,' she

said sincerely, wanting him to believe her.

'I think you mean that,' he said. 'At last I'm making an impression on you.'

You've already made it, Leslie thought wryly as they looked at each other.

'Now what's wrong?'

Leslie sighed. Gage interpreted each mood change. 'Nothing.'

'There had better not be, Miss Fletcher. Are you hungry?'

'Not really, but I wouldn't mind a cup of coffee.'

'I'll make some while you get comfortable. We have to share the bathroom.'

'I'm not a snob, Gage,' Leslie said impatiently.

He raised one eyebrow, shifted his long legs and left her alone.

Exhaling a deep breath, Leslie opened her brown suede suitcase and hung up the few articles of clothing she had brought with her. She took off her jacket, left it on the bed and went to join Gage in the kitchen.

'Sit down,' he offered.

Leslie sat down on one of the pine chairs and entwined her fingers in front of her on the table.

Gage poured coffee into a green mug from a stainless steel pot, his eyes on her hands. 'Don't tell me that the president is nervous.'

Leslie stopped wringing her hands together. 'Of course I'm not.'

Gage sat astride a chair. 'Look, Les. Right at this moment we're still on the same level. You're looking around, testing the situation. I'm open to negotiation. We have to remain calm.'

'I am calm.' But Leslie clutched the mug handle. Gage made her anything but calm.

'I'm not going to attack you. I'm not that type of guy.'

'I never even thought of it,' she said and she meant it.

'Good. At least you can judge my character. Now come on, drink up your coffee and we'll go for a walk around my estate.'

When they were ready, Leslie put on

141

her jacket and followed Gage outside. The undergrowth crackled beneath their feet as they walked, creating a mossy earthy aroma. Gage led Leslie along a forest path, closed in by small pine trees, until they reached an opening at the top of a hill. Below them and above them, snow-capped mountains soared, the luscious evergreens an umbrella beneath the blue sky.

'This is my favorite view,' Gage said enthusiastically. 'Did you ever think that there could be so many different shades of green in the trees?'

Leslie shook her head, awed. Trees climbed mountain peaks that she had no comprehension of defeating. 'The scenery makes me feel very small.'

'I guess that's why men try to destroy it. It gives them a sense of power.'

'I don't think they really meant to destroy it at first,' Leslie said. 'I think the destruction has escalated because of greed.'

'I couldn't have said that better myself,' Gage told her with approval.

'At least we're on the same wavelength.'

'For the time being,' Leslie said, not wanting to appear too vulnerable, but as she watched Gage silhouetted against the land, his shoulders broad and strong, his hips narrow above long muscular legs, her vulnerability increased as she welled with longing. Her heart turned over and over, and love for him seemed to enter every bone.

Gage's eyes were full of a blue glinting heat as he put out his hand. Leslie folded her fingers into his and moved toward him, knowing what was going to happen but powerless to stop the momentum. Her breath raced out of control; her pulse thudded as his hands cupped her face.

'What about business?' she stammered.

'To hell with it.'

Leslie knew she shouldn't respond to Gage like this if she were to keep her sanity, but her inhibitions were untamed. He ground his mouth against hers until she was spiraling into space.

She had to stop herself from drawing him closer, from arching against him, she needed his kisses so much. When his tongue invaded the soft cavern of her mouth, tasting of the fresh out-doors, she poked and teased with her own, enjoying this play immensely until her lips opened to taste all of him.

Gage's hands slid down her hips as he groaned her name. Her own hands clutched his back, her fingers pressed into his thick wool sweater.

'This is crazy,' she whispered.

'Crazy but necessary.' Again Gage's mouth covered hers. She could have escaped, she supposed, if she had wanted to escape, but the truth was she didn't. She had to feel his mouth, his tongue, the heightened breathing, the flush of hot emotion that lit her body. All around was the rustle of the breeze through the trees urging her on, the cool crisp pine-and-snow-mingled air, making her lightheaded. Fire sizzled along Leslie's veins as his hand rested over her breast. She closed her eyes and swayed.

'I could take you here,' Gage said roughly, his breath moist as his mouth settled close to her ear. His fingers gently rubbed over one hardened nipple. 'Do you want me, Les?'

She almost said yes. She nearly gave in, but a faint sharp whiff of sulfur caught the wind and pressed into her nostrils. It reminded her of why she was here. She wasn't on a pleasure trip with Gage. She was in Preston Falls on business. To go to bed with Gage could be her downfall. With determination, she slipped out of his arms.

For a long time he didn't say a word, until, 'How many times have I been rejected by you, Miss Fletcher?'

Leslie shook her head, denying the rejection. Desire throbbed in waves through her body, and her legs were so weak she wanted to sink into the grass, but she managed to plant her feet firmly on the ground. Gage was just as aroused. His face was flushed, his hands shaking as he smoothed his sweater to the waistline of his snug jeans. There were other signs, but she kept her eyes on his face.

'I don't think it's wise,' Leslie said huskily at last.

'Business again?' he questioned edgily.

'It's still there, Gage.'

'And it's certainly not going to go away,' he said bitterly. He thrust his hands in his pockets. 'We have to do something. Why don't we go for dinner at that little café on the marina?'

He was right. They did have to do something. Leslie nodded. 'That sounds nice.'

He turned and walked ahead of her. As Leslie followed close behind, she noticed how sure his booted feet were for such a large man. He was more than handsome and attractive — he was animal, aggressively male, yet kind and gentle. He stood apart, even while he blended into his surroundings. She could imagine him salvaging logs, the profession that had given him such empathy with his environment.

She accused him of being a tough bushman, and she was sure he could be that at times, but she could also see his sensitive side that gave him a knowledge of the world and made him very special.

Gage kicked off his muddy boots outside the front door, and Leslie did the same, not wanting to make his cottage dirty.

'Should we change clothes?' she asked, feeling awkward as she stood in the middle of his home. It was so much a part of him that she felt honored to be staying here.

'If you feel you want to,' Gage said, his eyes still holding a trace of blue passion.

'I'd like to, to . . . maybe put on a blouse.'

'Then go ahead.' He smiled.

His smile eased Leslie's discomfort, and she scurried into her bedroom and closed the door. She took off her jacket and pulled her sweater over her head. Gazing at herself in brown slacks and skin-toned bra, her breasts still flushed from arousal, she wondered how these strong emotions and feelings had suddenly happened to her. After being cold for so long, she felt as if she were melting.

She quickly buttoned on a cream silk blouse that had frills around the full sleeves and vee neckline. She wore her gold chain, and decided that brown heels looked presentable enough with the slacks. She didn't want to overdress for the town.

Hair brushed and mouth confident with coral lipstick, she returned to the living room. Gage was in his bedroom; she could hear him moving around so she amused herself by exploring. There were papers beside the typewriter which she longed to look at to see if it was his writing, but she didn't want to pry. The art on the wooden walls was all original native art, and she had a feeling that Gage would feel an affinity with the Indians in this part of the country. One painting, a small acrylic of a green and red bird, was signed personally to Gage.

His door opened, and she turned around abruptly. He was wearing black cords and a gray shirt, open at the neck. He shrugged on his leather jacket.

'Ready?' he asked.

Leslie slipped into her own jacket. 'Yes.'

As they climbed into the truck, he said, 'I'm sorry it's not a Cadillac.'

'Stop it, Gage,' Leslie said angrily. 'That wasn't the reason I withdrew from . . .'

'Our lovemaking,' he finished for her.

'Right,' she agreed. 'I don't look down on you. In fact, I rather respect you, but you have to see our positions.'

'Right now I'm seeing them in bed,' he told her.

She smiled slightly. 'We have to go beyond bed.'

'We will, Les,' he said. 'When all this is over, we're going to go a long way.'

A long way from each other, probably, Leslie thought, and she felt terribly sad.

Gage shook his head. 'Come close, let me put my arm around you.'

Leslie hesitated only a moment before she slipped across the seat. Gage placed his arm around her shoulders, a pose she had never tried in her high school years because Paul Fletcher had been so paranoid about her dating. Impulsively she reached up to clasp Gage's fingers.

He squeezed tightly, and they drove in silence through the town to the marina.

★   ★   ★

The waitress at the restaurant knew Gage and led them to a secluded table overlooking the harbor. The sun over the water reflected on the logs that bounced on the rolling blue waves, and the pine trees poked saucily into the sky. The entire scene was peaceful.

Leslie wanted to bring some of the peace to her relationship with Gage. She rested her slim hands on the wooden table. 'Tell me more about yourself,' she said.

'Like what?'

'Did you grow up here in Preston Falls, or in Vancouver?'

'I was born here. My father taught in the local school for a while until he got restless for the city. We moved when I was twelve.'

'Did you return right from university?'

Gage shook his head. 'No. I did my antiwar caper first.' He raised one dark blond eyebrow.

'It didn't work, though, did it? The world's still in a mess.'

'One war ends, another one starts,' Gage said.

Leslie moved her cutlery around on the table. She knew that he was also referring to their own war. But she wanted to forget about their problems for a while. 'Are you the only Preston left in town?'

'My uncle Mick's still around. All my ancestors were prospectors. Mick wanders around the country with his

151

Geiger counter, hoping to strike something. He never does anymore. It's a bit sad.'

'But I bet he wouldn't want to live anywhere else,' Leslie surmised.

'You're right. He's almost ninety and still spry.'

'Do you see yourself like that?' Leslie asked, her heart in her mouth. She had wondered once before what would happen if they could make a commitment to each other. Where would they live?

'I could end up like that, I suppose. Mick never married. I guess that's why he stayed. All the others met women and moved away.'

Would Gage move away? It was a question Leslie was loathe to put to him. She didn't want a definite answer. Luckily the waitress brought their order at that moment.

Leslie was ravenous after only having a cup of coffee for lunch and foregoing breakfast before traveling. She joined Gage in sampling the delicious steaks, baked potatoes with creamy butter, followed by dessert of blueberry pie and ice cream. When they left the restaurant, she felt full.

'I think I'll explode. The food was great, Gage.'

'The restaurant was built for the people in the houses on the hill. It caters to the elite.'

Leslie glanced at his profile as they walked to the truck. 'Why are you so cynical?'

'Because it's the truth. Most of the residents feel that they wouldn't be welcome in that place.'

'But you still go there,' she argued. 'You could go to the restaurant in town if you wanted to.'

'I go there as well.'

Leslie lifted her shoulders at his stubborn streak. 'I give up.'

'But I wouldn't take you to the one in town,' Gage said.

'You didn't have to take me any-where,' she snapped before walking down to the edge of the marina. The night sea breeze blew through her hair and cooled her skin.

She tensed as Gage's fingers clasped her shoulders. His mouth pressed warmly against her neck. 'We couldn't stay at the cottage,' he said huskily. His hands slipped down her arms. 'You know that, Les.'

She nodded, feeling cold as his hands dropped from her.

'Come on, get in the truck,' he said.

Leslie sat apart from Gage as he started the engine. She thought he would drive directly home, but she found they were going along a road around the edge of the water.

'We'll have a great view of the sunset here,' he said as he parked by a beach. 'How's this?'

'Do you swim here?' Leslie asked because it was the only thing she could think of to say.

'I have.' Gage smiled slightly. 'It's a bit cool tonight for skinny dipping.'

'I wasn't thinking about that.'

'No?'

Leslie shook her head.

His hand stroked the steering wheel. 'I was thinking about us being naked together.'

Leslie closed her eyes. 'Don't, Gage.'

'I can't help it. I've been wanting you from the minute I laid eyes on you, and I'm going to have you, Leslie Fletcher.'

'It's foolish.'

Gage put his hand on her shoulder and tugged her closer. 'A lot of things in life are foolish, but they're fun.'

'Is that all it's going to be, a game?' Leslie knew she sounded panic stricken. If she made love with Gage it would be for life.

He ran his mouth down the side of her soft cheek to the edge of her trembling mouth. 'No games.'

Leslie tried to pay attention to the sun setting over the horizon of ocean and trees, but it was difficult with Gage so near. Red fingers of light drowned them as she let him tease her tremulous lips, then brush her throat, nibble her chin, caress her cheeks, tickle her eyes with his lashes . . .

Leslie giggled, and Gage hugged her. 'Isn't it good?'

'Yes,' she agreed.

He drew back before lowering his mouth to hers once more. Leslie joined her tongue with his, entwining, enjoying, abandoning herself to the sensations that drifted silkily through her body. His hands restlessly stroked over her blouse.

'Let's go home,' he whispered.

His eyes, as blue as the ocean, were persuading her, evoking a longing deep inside her, emotions that needed easing as she knew only Gage could ease them. When Leslie thought of the adventure that was to come, she burned.

One small light glowed outside the cottage in the dense darkness of the forest night. Gage helped Leslie out of the truck, leading her across the grassy terrain and up the steps to the veranda. When Leslie nearly stumbled in the dusky light, Gage put his strong arm around her waist and she felt him kiss her hair.

In the dark silence of the cottage, Leslie turned into his arms as if it were natural. She grazed her soft mouth against his rough cheek.

'Don't stop,' he muttered.

She had to touch him, taste him . . . she buried her face into his neck and he tangled his fingers into her hair, drawing it aside to caress her skin with his warm mouth. Leslie's body ached with need for him, and she was fast losing control as she'd never lost control before. Her body seemed to be running away from her mind.

When Gage pulled back she felt cool, but he wrapped her hand securely in his to take her into his bedroom. The open curtains outlined the full moon and Gage against the window. Leslie knew that she would always remember Gage as a cut-out against the forest — whatever happened.

She also knew that her feelings were love. She loved Gage with a passion she had never felt for any other man. She wanted his touch, his lovemaking. She needed the full force of his strong body against her.

Her desires communicated to Gage because he moved forward to cover her mouth with his. Earlier the kisses had been softer, more teasing, but now his lips were demanding, almost frightening in intensity. His hands slipped over her body and he molded her against his chest and thighs.

Leslie felt his eagerness and although her own arousal soared from his nearness, it disturbed her to know what he could do to her. Not only physically, but emotionally.

Gage felt her stiffen and stopped kissing her. 'Did I hurt you?'

Not yet, she thought, but one day he might. Right now she still had a minimum control over her body and emotions. If she slept with Gage, she would be his.

Gage's fingers slipped shakily down her arms, his eyes dark and fathomless.

'Pulling out?' he asked thickly.

Leslie nodded, not trusting herself to speak.

Gage cupped her face in his hands. 'Okay, but I will have you, Les. One day. Now run along.'

7

The delicious aroma of bacon and eggs woke Leslie in the morning. She sat up in bed wondering where she was, while the partly open window let in the scent of pine trees joining the cottage's own woody smell seeping from the pores of the timber. She fumbled on the bedside table for her watch to check the time.

She had to get up and dressed for her meeting with Cliff Daniels down at the Fletcher Paper mill. It reminded her clearly of why she was here in Preston Falls, and although an edge of frustration and longing still remained with her for Gage, she was glad that she had been strong enough to turn him down.

But not because I don't love you, my darling, she thought. She wondered if her father had ever felt that way about her, but hadn't mentioned his feelings because of lack of time or the appropriate moment. Humans do hurt each other. She sighed and got out of bed.

Dressed in her blue velour robe, she took designer jeans and a white silk shirt and matching underwear from her suitcase. Rolling the clothes beneath her arm, she picked up her toilet bag and walked through to the bathroom.

Gage was standing at the stove cooking when she passed the kitchen, so she said good morning a little shyly.

'Good morning to you,' Gage said with a slight smile.

His smile relaxed Leslie. It intimated no hard feelings, and she was pleased. Gage might not like rejection, but at least he handled himself maturely.

'I'm going to use the bathroom,' Leslie told him, feeling she had to speak.

'Go ahead, the cottage is yours. Breakfast will be ready when you are.'

Leslie dressed, washed and combed her hair before returning her robe to the bedroom. She joined Gage in the kitchen.

'Pour yourself some orange juice,' he told her, indicating a pitcher on the table.

Leslie did as she was told, finding the juice was made from fresh oranges. She sat down and Gage served her two eggs, bacon and toast.

'I'm not used to eating all this,' she said, but ate hungrily.

Gage chuckled. 'No, but you're doing a pretty good job.'

'It must be all the fresh air.'

'Probably,' he agreed, and attacked his own breakfast.

But Leslie could feel the atmosphere tensing between them even though Gage was acting so casually. It was like being in a web of tight rubberbands. If one snapped the entire web would collapse.

Leslie knew the causes. Sexual strain was high between them, but there was also this morning's meeting at the mill. The results would be crucial to the direction of their future — personal and business — relationship.

'I'll drive you downtown,' Gage said as he cleared his plate.

Leslie smiled slightly. 'Downtown?'

He looked wry. 'Well. I'll drop into the hotel for a beer while you go to the mill.'

'Okay,' she said, and went to get her purse, briefcase and jacket.

★   ★   ★

Cliff Daniels's office was littered with papers, over-flowing file cabinets, a desk and chairs. An antique black typewriter stood on a corner table, and Leslie wondered if it was an indication of the age of all the equipment in the mill. As she glanced around at the scratched green walls and well-worn green floor tiles, she felt guilt for her own luxurious office.

She had never been made so aware of her own power. The brunette secretary hurriedly brought her coffee in a mug instead of the styrofoam cups everyone else seemed to use, and Cliff Daniels, portly and bald, smiled nervously as he pumped her hand.

'This is a surprise, you know, Miss Fletcher. We were all sorry about your father.'

'Thank you,' Leslie said politely, trying to get the man to relax. 'I think I should have visited a long time ago.'

'Well, at least you're here now. Did you want a tour of the mill?'

'I'd like as much information on the operation and equipment as I can get,' Leslie told him, taking the yellow hardhat he offered.

'Follow me, then,' Cliff told her, and led her along a corridor out into the plant.

'We only make newsprint at this mill,' Cliff continued, letting her feel the grainy texture of a sheet of paper. 'But you probably know that.' He laughed nervously.

Leslie smiled and shook her head. 'I don't know much at all. Just tell me everything you know.'

Her modesty seemed to please Cliff as he went into a detailed explanation of the pulp and paper process. 'There are two methods of making pulp: the mechanical or groundwood method where the logs are ground by large revolving grinders; or there is the chemical pulp, where the wood is chipped, not ground. The chips are cooked in chemicals dissolving the lignin, which is the natural glue that holds the wood fibers together. To make newsprint we blend the chemical and groundwood pulp together, because groundwood on its own doesn't make good paper. We blend them on one of these draining screens.' Cliff pointed to the equipment. 'They are called four-driniers. They move into the paper-making machine where the drained pulp is fed through a drying section. See here, it looks like wet felt.'

Leslie nodded. 'What kind of wood do you use as raw material?'

'Low-grade stuff, or waste wood from the plywood and lumber mills.'

'How long does the paper-making process take?'

'Ten seconds from the time the blended pulp moves on to the four-drinier. The newsprint comes out at a rate of half a mile a minute.'

'A quick process.' Leslie smiled. She stepped back from the noise slightly. 'Is this equipment outdated?'

Cliff shrugged. 'Well . . . yes, to be truthful. This is only a small mill.'

'I realize that, but do you feel it's safe?'

'It breaks down a lot and we're continuously losing time by making repairs. We have had a few accidents.'

'Maybe you can give me more details in your office,' Leslie told him.

When they returned to Cliff's office, he ordered more coffee, cleared a space on his cluttered desk and worked with Leslie, giving her the information she requested.

As Leslie took down details and was given reports and copies of invoices, she realized that although Cliff worked in disorganization, his mind was clear and lucid, and he had every fact at his fingertips.

When they had finished, Leslie filled her briefcase with all the papers she had accumulated. 'You've really helped me a lot,' she told Cliff sincerely.

'You obviously have a reason for your visit.' Cliff seemed much more relaxed now.

'Do you know Gage Preston?' she asked.

'Of course. Is he making trouble again?'

'Has he made trouble in the past?' Leslie asked cautiously.

'He's strictly for the environment,' Cliff said. 'Although he has a lot of bargaining power. Peter Slater, the union head, is on his side.'

'And that means he has the cooperation of the mill workers,' Leslie said perceptively.

'You're absolutely right. I'm not against their demands, but when you're on management, as you well know, you have to be cautious. You can't give in indiscriminately.'

'But you do feel there is a need for safer working conditions?'

'Definitely,' Cliff said. 'And if you can see that in Vancouver and help us out, then all the better.'

'Are you willing to let Gage be your spokesman?'

Cliff nodded. 'I've known Gage a long time. He means well and he's dedicated.'

'You realize that it's more than safer working conditions. He wants pollution controls put on the mill,' Leslie said.

'Yes,' Cliff said. 'I guess we all worry about our water supply.'

'I want to do something,' Leslie said sincerely. 'But I have a strong board to contend with. This mill isn't a very large operation. If the cost for updating equipment and pollution controls is more than the profits they might even suggest closure.'

Leslie noticed Cliff swallow hard, and she now knew why he had never rocked the boat too hard. He knew the probable consequences.

'I don't want that,' Leslie continued. 'So I'm going to have to go carefully. You're right, management does have to be cautious.'

'Preston Falls needs the mill,' Cliff said. 'If it closes down, this will probably become some vacation resort for the rich, or the town will die.'

'I understand.' Leslie stood up, feeling she had taken up enough of the man's time. 'I'll let you know what happens. I'm negotiating with Gage.'

'He's a strong nut.' Cliff smiled as he shook her hand. 'He's stubborn when he thinks he's right.'

'I know.' Leslie returned his smile. 'Thank you for everything.'

'You're welcome.' Cliff walked her to the main entrance. 'I was pleased to have you visit. It makes us feel closer.'

★　★　★

As Leslie walked down the main street of town, she noticed Gage's brown truck parked outside the hotel. Squaring her shoulders, because the entrance smelled like a brewery, she walked inside and followed the sign to the bar.

Gage sat at a small round table.

'You shouldn't be in here,' he said, not looking up.

'I've been in a bar before,' Leslie said softly, taking a seat. 'Are you going to order me a drink?'

With a resigned shrug, Gage ordered another beer. 'So how did it go?'

'Fine. I learned how a paper mill works and saw the equipment with my own eyes.'

'If you sold it off, you'd probably make a fortune on the antique market,' Gage said wryly.

'It is old,' she agreed.

'But you're not passing any judgment as yet,' Gage reflected.

She nodded, and sipped her drink.

'Very astute, Miss Fletcher, but just remember we're dealing with the fact that we want a world worth passing on to our children.'

'I won't forget,' she said quietly, her eyes meeting his through the low light.

'You do care, don't you, Les?' he asked.

'Yes, I do,' she admitted.

'Good.' He stood up. 'Let's get out of this place.'

★   ★   ★

'Did you meet Peter Slater when you were at the mill?' Gage asked as they drove back to his cottage.

'No, I didn't. Just Cliff,' Leslie told him. 'Do you think I should meet him?'

'You'll be dealing with him if things deteriorate.'

Leslie sighed. 'Well, let's hope that the board considers my proposal, but maybe I should meet Peter.'

'I usually drop over for dinner with them on Friday nights. I was talking to Molly, his wife, and she invited you along.'

171

'Okay,' Leslie said, realizing that it would mean another night at Gage's cottage. 'If you don't mind flying me back home tomorrow morning. My mother's having a little get-together Saturday night. I've promised to attend.'

'That's fine,' Gage said. 'I'd like to meet your mother.'

Leslie couldn't help laughing. 'In other words you want me to invite you along?'

'If you invite me to meet your mother, I'll take you out to meet my family on Sunday for the day.'

Leslie raised one eyebrow. She had never been organized so thoroughly before in her life, but she rather liked it. It would mean she would be with Gage for the entire weekend.

'Okay?' Gage asked.

Leslie nodded, pushing away any dark thoughts that in a few weeks this friendship and budding romance might be shattered into a revolution.

★   ★   ★

When they arrived back at the cottage, Gage suggested packing a lunch and going for a hike. Leslie, who hadn't hiked since her European trip, agreed.

Gage strapped a knapsack to his back and led the way through forest trails that he seemed to know blindfolded. Glad of her comfortable boots and jeans, Leslie followed, letting the damp spring breeze blow through her hair and on her face. She was amazed at how content and peaceful she felt despite the storm that was brewing offstage between herself and Gage. There was something about Gage's presence that stopped any extra longing. Loneliness was a thing of the past.

Gage stopped in a mossy clearing and eased the knapsack off his back. 'Tired?' he asked.

'Not really,' Leslie said truthfully. 'I'm enjoying myself.'

'Then the forest doesn't scare you?'

'Why should it scare me?'

'It bothers some people,' Gage remarked. He made himself comfortable on a patch of grass and patted the space beside him. 'Come and sit down.'

Gage had packed thick cheese slices between rye bread, small sweet tomatoes and cans of beer. As they ate, Gage transferred some of his knowledge of the trees and plants to Leslie. He picked up a large pine cone. 'Don't you think that's a tremendous piece of work?'

'Yes,' she agreed, handling the spiky cone, feeling as if she were touching Gage himself because his love of nature was so strong. She tucked the cone in her pocket. 'I'm going to keep it.'

His blue eyes raked her face, the streaky sun lighting up his hair. 'Why?'

'Because I want to remember you here . . . ' she told him shyly.

His fingertips were slightly rough as he stroked her face. 'Why did you stop last night?'

Leslie felt the vibrations begin again. Longing pressed through her body. 'It would only complicate matters if we . . . '

'Went to bed?' he finished.

Leslie nodded, her brown eyes luminous in the shaded forest light.

Gage bent forward and stroked her lips with his. 'Your mouth trembles when I touch you.'

Everything trembles, she thought, knowing she should move away from him, but her body wouldn't let her. She put up her hand and brushed her fingers through his curly hair, and sank with him into the soft grass.

Gage's thighs rested against hers, and she could feel his passion rising along with her own. She arched her hips and moaned beneath his steady kisses.

'You reject me, but you don't want to reject me,' Gage told her breathlessly.

'It has nothing to do with rejection.' Leslie wanted to reassure him.

Gage rolled away from her and gazed restlessly at the white clouds that drifted through the sky. 'It sure feels like it,' he said.

Leslie felt suddenly cold. Were man/woman relationships always so complicated? They seemed to travel in circles when they should be going in a straight line. She shifted to her side, and drew her legs up slightly.

She stayed like that for a long time. Gage lay beside her. The wind rustled the branches of the trees around them. Leslie felt she should say something. 'I'm sorry.'

'Ah, don't start that,' he said. 'Sex has to be mutual. If you're psychologically not ready, then it won't work.' He sat up and dragged the knapsack to his side, stuffing in the remains of their lunch. 'Come on, let's get back. We don't want to be late for dinner.'

The hike back wasn't as peaceful as on the journey out. Leslie could sense that Gage was disgruntled and she felt sad that there had to be a barrier between them. She would like to think that if she weren't president of Fletcher Paper she would be Gage's lover by now.

But she found out that Gage wasn't a man to hold a grudge. When they reached the cottage and had disposed of their muddy boots on the veranda, he reached over and tousled Leslie's curly hair.

'Hey, don't look so sad.'

'I thought you were mad at me,' she said cautiously.

'No.' He grinned. 'Just getting to know you.'

'That bad, eh?'

'All humans are complex, Les. You're no exception. I find you more interesting than most, that's all. Now run along, make yourself pretty for tonight.'

Leslie did as he said. In her bedroom, she tucked the pine cone in the corner of her suitcase.

★   ★   ★

Leslie wore her tan slacks and matching silk shirt blouse, and swept her hair into a mass of curls on top of her head for dinner at the Slaters. As she pushed her feet into brown high heels and checked her reflection once more in the dresser mirror, she felt self-assured.

Gage, wearing gray dress pants and a blue shirt, popped his head around the door. 'Ready?' he asked.

Leslie nodded. 'Yes.'

'You look nice,' he complimented.

'So do you.' Leslie smiled slightly, wondering what it would be like if this man were her husband. She would be with him forever like this, and the thought was very appealing. No more loneliness, always Gage.

Gage gave her a friendly wink. 'Get your jacket.'

The outskirts of Preston Falls were clustered with suburban houses. As Gage parked the truck in the driveway alongside two other cars, Leslie felt that the low ranch-style stucco house with its long green lawns and pretty flowers looked incongruous sitting in a bowl of dense, rough bush. Two teenage boys were sprawled on the lawn, fiddling with a ten-speed bicycle.

'Hi, Gage,' one of them said, gray eyes giving Leslie's figure the once-over.

'Hi, Paul. Hi, Randall. Won't your wheels work?'

'No,' Paul groaned. 'Dad's too cheap to buy us a car.'

'Cars are pretty expensive nowadays,' Gage said, softening the remark with a grin. 'Boys, this is Leslie Fletcher. Paul and Randall Slater, Les.'

'Anything to do with the mill?' Randall asked curiously.

'The president,' Gage said.

'Oh, yeah,' the boys chorused disbelievingly as Gage nudged Leslie up to the front door.

Gage laughed close to her ear. 'They didn't believe me.'

'It's because I'm a woman,' she said jokingly. 'Seeds of male chauvinism are even planted in the young.'

'You could be right,' Gage agreed. 'It doesn't bother me that you're a woman.'

'We wouldn't have our problem if I weren't,' Leslie remarked.

Gage dropped a light kiss on the side of her neck. 'That's for sure.' He rang the doorbell.

'Gage, I'm so glad you could come.' Molly Slater, gray eyes shining, gave Gage a hug.

Gage introduced Leslie, who was treated to a handshake from the slim woman in blue slacks, matching blouse and soft gray hair. 'Come on in. Peter will get you drinks while I put the finishing touches on the meal. I hope you like roast pork, Miss Fletcher.'

'I love it,' Leslie told Molly as they entered the house. The foyer was cluttered with books, sports equipment, shoes and clothes.

'You'll have to excuse the mess,' Molly said. 'With three teenagers and a job, I can't keep up with the tidying.'

'Don't worry,' Leslie said, noticing Gage's amusement as he looked at her reaction to the Slaters' house. He was expecting her to be a snob about everything. 'Please call me Leslie,' she told Molly.

'Okay, I will. I just didn't know.'

Gage whispered to Leslie, 'She would never have called your father Paul.'

'Neither would I,' Leslie retorted and Gage grinned.

Leslie found Peter Slater as charming as his wife, and the dinner turned into a tale-telling affair. It was as if Fletcher Paper and the problems didn't exist as Gage and Peter traded logging stories. Molly obviously had accompanied her husband through all his experiences, and she added some of the humor to the incidents, which led to a teasing backchat between husband and wife.

Leslie could see that they had a very stable relationship and the difference between her parent's marriage was painful to her. Molly was as strong as Peter, and no one put her down. Leslie had always avoided thinking about marriage, but now it was pushing into the forefront with Gage as her prospective partner.

But it might never happen, she thought sadly as she took a seat in the comfortable living room for their coffee.

Peter Slater sat down beside her. 'I'm

glad we could meet,' he said.

'So am I.' Leslie smiled, but she realized that behind Peter's casual attitude was a shrewd mind. He was weighing her up as a person, possibly a force to contend with. He also eyed Gage a few times as if seeing his friend in a new light. Did he wonder about Gage's relationship with her?

Leslie glanced across at the man who had invaded her life. He was explaining something to Molly, and he looked intense, as if he truly believed in what he was saying. Which he probably did, Leslie thought. She had the feeling that once Gage loved a woman, she would get his entire attention. A little stifling for some women maybe, but Leslie knew that for her it would be all she ever dreamed of.

Keep dreaming, Les, she thought wryly, and turned back to Peter's conversation. She would have to put Gage Preston on a shelf for the time being.

But it wasn't easy. Driving home in

the pitch blackness of the forest night with only the truck's headlights to guide the way, Leslie slipped across the seat into Gage's curved arm.

He caressed her shoulder. 'Have a good time?'

'Very. The Slaters are nice people.'

'Molly's got Peter where she wants him now,' Gage remarked.

'Oh, I didn't think that. I thought they were pretty equal.'

'Maybe they are,' Gage agreed. 'Peter comes on easygoing, but he has his hard side. Maybe Molly had to fight to stop him dominating her.'

'Fighting was something my mother didn't do,' Leslie commented.

Gage's eyes twinkled in the low light. 'Unlike her daughter.'

'Do you think I'm a fighter?'

'Oh, definitely.'

'Do you mind?'

'No, it's a challenge.'

Leslie focused on his profile. 'So you look on women as challenges?'

'Did I say that?' Gage laughed.

'Now, don't get out of it,' Leslie said. 'You must have had a lot of women because you never got married again.'

'I never got married again because I didn't fall in love,' he said. 'Simple explanation.'

'But the other night you said all your women had been true lovers.'

'Did I say that?' Gage chuckled.

'Don't tease me, Gage. What did you mean?'

'Just what I said. I cared, but not enough to wake up with them for the rest of my life.'

'Then you used them.'

'No, I didn't. At the time I felt love. Leslie, this is getting complicated.'

'Love seems very complicated,' she remarked.

Gage stopped the truck outside the cottage, then squeezed her shoulder. 'It is complicated, but you'll get the hang of it.'

Before Leslie could answer him, he'd slipped out the truck, slammed his door, opened hers and helped her onto the grass. They walked into the cottage.

Leslie knew she should go straight to her bedroom, but all the talk of Gage's other women had unsettled her. Jealousy was a churning lump inside her.

But Gage didn't seem to have any patience with her. 'Go to bed, Les,' he said.

She couldn't argue with his set features. She bid him goodnight and did as she was told. But as she leaned against the closed door, her heart twisted painfully.

8

Living with Gage could become a comfortable habit, Leslie thought as she drifted awake the following morning, listening to him move around in his kitchen. Gone was the jealousy of the evening before. She only wanted to see him again.

But after enthusiastically dressing in jeans and a loose maroon sweatshirt, she slowed herself down and walked cautiously into the kitchen.

'Morning,' she said cheerfully.

'Good morning.' Gage smiled slightly at her bare feet and tousled hair.

Leslie helped herself to a glass of orange juice and cupped her hands around it. 'What time are we leaving?'

'As soon as we're ready. Do you want a full breakfast, or will toast do?'

'Toast sounds good,' Leslie told him. She leaned against the edge of the table and watched him. He wore faded jeans and a black T-shirt. On his feet were a pair of gray work socks, and Leslie thought they made him look vulnerable. Her heart turned over.

'Toast.' Gage put a plate of buttered toast in front of her.

Leslie sat down and waited for Gage to join her. They ate in silence, finishing the toast, drinking orange juice and coffee.

'This is a good restaurant,' Leslie said when she'd finished, feeling she had to say something.

'I've enjoyed having you here,' Gage told her and stood up. 'Why don't you go pack your bags. We'll get going.'

Once again Leslie was ordered by Gage to go to her room. But as she packed, she felt sad. This cottage would make a perfect hideaway for lovers.

★ ★ ★

For her mother's party, Leslie chose a black crepe dress with long sleeves and

187

a low vee neckline, to which she added a diamond brooch in a spray of leaves at her breast. She left her hair loose and curly and made up her eyes. Her skin had gained a slight blush from being outdoors over the last few days, and she didn't need further makeup. High-heeled black sandals added to her height and she was mentally prepared by the time Gage rang her doorbell.

He was more relaxed than he had been earlier that day, and Leslie wondered if the dress-up clothes made a difference. In his silver gray suit that rippled over his body, he looked as if he could conquer the world.

Leslie expected Gage to comment on the white marble pillars at her mother's house, but he just parked the car and walked with her up the wide steps.

Betty showed them through to the living room where a group circulated, drinking and nibbling on tasty seafood hors d'oeuvres.

Leslie was delighted at her mother's reaction to Gage. She could see that

Caroline was stunned that her daughter would present such a serious man, but her well-ingrained social graces kept her from showing her surprise.

'How wonderful to meet you,' Caroline said, shaking Gage's hands.

Gage gave Caroline one of his most charming smiles. 'And I'm pleased to meet you, Mrs. Fletcher.'

'Call me Caroline.' Leslie's mother fluttered her dark eyelashes.

The reaction from the rest of her mother's friends was the same. They had long given up on Leslie marrying, and were duly impressed with Gage. So impressed that Leslie lost touch with him for most of the evening. Exhausted from so much social posturing, she escaped to the food table. She picked up a jumbo shrimp, dipped it in tangy seafood sauce and nibbled. Popping it into her mouth, she dipped another one. They were good, she thought, wiping her hands on a dainty yellow cocktail napkin. She spotted Gage talking to her mother, and he noticed her, closing one eye in a wink.

Leslie smiled and raised her dark brown eyebrows. But as Gage bent forward to speak to her mother again, the smile abruptly faded. Easy rapport with Gage was a trap she could get into. No matter how much she loved him, she had to be practical about the future of such action.

'You look sad.' Warm breath fluttered the curls around her ear.

Gage's fingers rested lightly and warmly on her waist. 'Your mother thinks I'm a very nice man.'

'Some people aren't very good judges of character,' Leslie said cheekily, glad to feel that the day's tension had receded.

'Don't you think I'm a nice man?' Gage prodded.

'Nice maybe, but . . . ' Leslie rolled velvet brown eyes at him.

'Is this teasing or a putdown?' he asked.

'Teasing.' Leslie rested her fingers briefly on his arm.

He glanced down at her hand. 'I like it when you touch me, Leslie.'

Her fingertips pressed harder into the smooth suit material and she felt his muscles contract. She rubbed upwards, not being able to stop herself, vibrations echoing through her own arm.

'When's that proposal going to the board?' Gage asked roughly, suddenly.

'A week, maybe two,' Leslie told him.

'When it's over, Les, we have to make a decision to have a commitment.'

'It might never be over.' The words strained from Leslie's throat.

'Make it over,' Gage said firmly. 'You have the power.'

Did she have the power? Leslie thought of her stern board members, and wondered how much pull she really had with those men. Right now she felt as if she were on a pinnacle and everyone was waiting for her to either fall or stay upright.

★ ★ ★

191

Richard and Pearl Preston lived in a small English-style cottage overlooking a river ravine lot outside the city of Vancouver. Covered with ivy and flowers, the home was the perfect retirement refuge.

Leslie liked Gage's parents immediately. Easy to talk to, his mother was a gray-haired upright woman in jeans and a yellow shirt, and his father, also gray-haired, was an older, bulkier version of Gage. He had a little gray moustache which he liked to stroke as he talked, and Leslie could imagine him being a schoolteacher.

Gage's sister, Penny, and her husband, Mike, arrived halfway through the morning. Penny's two boys were carbon copies of their mother, with the same abundant curly gold hair. Mike was the odd one out — tall, dark, slim and quiet. Leslie learned that Penny and Mike were both schoolteachers.

To Leslie, whose family life had always been very sedate, she found the Preston home bordering on chaos.

Penny's conversation always turned into lectures while everyone teased, saying, 'Yes, Penny,' or 'Yes, Mother.'

As it was a warm sunny day, the children played on the swing and slide that doting grandparents had installed for their visits.

'We live in an apartment,' Penny confided to Leslie as they relaxed in patio chairs to watch Mike and Gage play an energetic game of badminton on the lawn. 'The kids go wild when they get to this house.'

'They seem pretty well-behaved,' Leslie remarked, watching Gage's mother catch Davey, the younger boy, at the bottom of the slide. Ronnie was having a piggy-back ride from his grandfather.

Penny gazed affectionately at her children. 'Sometimes.' She laughed. 'So what do you do for a living, Leslie?'

Leslie hesitated before saying, 'I work in an office.'

'Oh, we're all slotted into boxes, aren't we? I sometimes envy Gage his freedom. Have you been up to Preston Falls?'

'Yes,' Leslie said.

Penny continued probing. 'Then you've stayed at Gage's cottage?'

'Just for a couple of nights,' Leslie told her, knowing what it sounded like. Penny would think that Leslie was one of Gage's girlfriends.

'Hey, don't blush,' Penny said gently. 'Gage doesn't bring lady friends home very often. You must be a little special.'

'Has he had many girlfriends?' Leslie asked, wanting to know all about the man she loved.

'Not many. He had a pretty rough deal with his marriage. His wife went off with someone else.'

'She must have had a good reason.'

'She was a flirt, but she also didn't like what Gage was into at the time. He's been a bit of an activist, but he means well. He wants to save the world.'

'At least his little corner,' Leslie commented as Gage returned the badminton birdie with a forceful slice of the racket.

Penny laughed. 'Has he told you about Preston Falls? He's got some idea about tackling the paper company up there. Personally, I don't think he's got a chance in hell. Corporations turn a blind eye to that type of thing.'

Leslie tensed. 'He might find some-one compassionate, who believes in his cause.' She felt she had to defend herself, even if Penny didn't know she was doing it.

'Maybe.' Penny sighed. 'Anyway, it'll be good food for his novel. Did he tell you he was writing one?'

'He's mentioned it.'

'He'll do it. He has a lot of discipline, and he usually achieves what he wants from life.'

'Except his cause at Preston Falls,' Leslie said.

'Well, that's a pretty big meal he's put on his plate,' his sister said. 'But you never know. He might find a way to get through to them.'

Like having the president of the company in love with him, Leslie thought. Had she been coerced into a trap so Gage could get his own way, or had Gage been honest with her? She would like to believe it was the latter. It was something she didn't want to dwell on until after the crucial board meeting.

Mike tossed his badminton racket at Leslie. 'You play your boyfriend.' He grinned. 'I can't beat him.'

Leslie took the racket and walked over to Gage. 'Do you want to play me?' she asked.

'Always, Les,' he said softly, slightly out of breath. 'But you're at the advantage, you realize. You're rested up.'

'And I once won a badminton championship,' she told him cheekily, moving to her side of the net.

Leslie won the first game, then Gage the second, Leslie the third, Gage the fourth.

'Five-game match,' Gage shouted to her, obviously exhausted.

'You're on,' Leslie yelled back. She hadn't had so much fun in years. It was as if all her inhibitions had been let loose and she felt free.

She beat Gage, and the Preston family went mad.

'Good for you.' Gage's father patted her shoulder. 'Gage always thinks he's a winner.'

'But I'm a good loser.' Gage grinned and lifted Leslie into his arms. He planted a firm, sweaty kiss on her mouth. 'Congratulations,' he whispered. 'You're ahead one round.'

He would have to bring it back to work, Leslie thought, her spirits dimming slightly. But it kept everything in perspective. This happy time between them was a short reprieve.

* * *

As they drove home into Vancouver, Gage asked Leslie if she had enjoyed herself.

'Very much,' she said truthfully. 'I

like your family.'

He grinned sideways. 'My little office worker. Why did you tell Penny that?'

'People react differently to me when they know who I am.'

'So you're ashamed of being a Fletcher?'

'I didn't say that. I just don't want to appear superior.'

'Do you feel superior?' Gage asked.

'No.' Leslie sighed, and turned to look at the street and the flashing lights of the city.

It wasn't late, and Leslie felt she should invite Gage in for coffee. He lounged on her sofa, checking the panoramic view while she made coffee in the kitchen. She put the tray on the table near him.

'Thanks,' he said, and Leslie realized that he had been silent since the interchange in the car.

She sat down beside him. 'Gage. I didn't mean that I felt superior to your family. I enjoyed Penny's friendship, and I didn't want to change her attitude toward me.'

'I know.' Gage smiled to relax her. 'I'm just not very certain of you sometimes. I feel there might be a disdain for people a class or two below.'

'I've told you I'm not a snob, Gage.'

'I believe you.' He traced her features with his forefinger. Then he rested his forehead against hers. 'I've had such a good time this weekend.'

'Me too,' she said softly, nuzzling against him.

Leslie prepared herself for Gage's kiss by inhaling a deep breath, but she wasn't ready for the onslaught of emotions that careened through her. She felt as if she were on a bridge ready to jump. She swayed to him and pressed her mouth to his. She held his head with her hands, her fingertips exploring his ears, his strong neck, his broad shoulders. Restlessly they moved closer.

Gage lifted her onto his knees, and it reminded her of the day he'd kissed her on the plaza. He held off caressing her, but devastated her with his lips.

When Gage withdrew, his blue eyes were blazing. 'It's so hard for me not to love you,' he whispered. 'Touch me, Les.'

She did as he said, her hands softly stroking his chest. Boldly she unbuttoned the top of his shirt, and slipped her palm inside. His chest hair was crisp, his skin smooth and vital, the beat of his heart suffocating.

'Les,' he groaned. 'I have to have you.'

'I know,' she murmured as his mouth touched hers again. He cupped her breasts, brushing her nipples with his thumbs until Leslie arched into him, aching for more.

'You want me?'

It was a question, posed in a hoarse, passion-filled voice, and all Leslie could do was nod. One day she had to make love, and why not with Gage, the man she loved.

He stood up, carrying her in his arms. Slightly apprehensive nonetheless, Leslie cuddled against him, her arms entwined around his neck.

He seemed to know the bedroom instinctively, and gently lowered Leslie to the bed. He followed her down, his mouth eager against hers, his thighs pressing her into the oyster silk.

While he was kissing her, Leslie could feel expert male fingers working on her shirt buttons. He tossed her blouse and bra aside before gazing at her breasts.

'Beautiful,' he murmured, savoring the tips with his tongue until Leslie thought she was going mad. Feelings she had never experienced before rushed from her toes to her brain. She gasped out loud when he unbuttoned her jeans.

'Take your shirt off,' she said huskily, wanting to stall him for a moment. She needed more time to get used to what they were doing.

Gage did as she asked, amusement curving his mouth while passion burned in his eyes, in the slight flare of his nostrils, as he restrained his emotions.

Leslie knew that what he felt for her was as raw and untamed as the emotion she was experiencing. Only he knew how to handle it.

She reached up and stroked his chest, her fingertips tingling. Slightly embarrassed beneath his hot eyes, she turned her head into the soft silk pillow.

'Watch me, Les,' Gage said thickly. 'I want you so much.'

Leslie forced herself to look at him and when she did she couldn't keep her eyes off him. She drank in every line of his rough-hewn features, his broad shoulders, the tan that spread golden down his chest to his waist. Her heart thudded in her head as Gage moved beside her, and the effect of his skin touching hers made her shudder.

Wildfire was leaping through her veins, but she was also tense. As his fingers, slightly rough at the tips, slowly meandered over her thighs, she convulsed with a sob of despair.

Gage stroked her back gently. 'Okay,

Les,' he said. 'It's nothing to be ashamed of.'

'How do you know?'

'Experience.' Gage sighed. 'Why didn't you tell me?'

'I was embarrassed.' Leslie looked up at him, clutching the silk sheet with restless fingers. 'I'm twenty-eight, Gage. In this day and age it's ridiculous.'

'So you pretended you were worldly?'

'Yes.'

He shook his head. 'Do you want to tell me why?'

'When I was a teenager I wasn't allowed to date, and I think it gave me a hangup. Since then, I've never felt I wanted any of the men I've gone out with.'

'Did your father stop you dating?'

'Only the men I really liked.'

'What about when you went to Europe?'

'I couldn't let myself go, even though Suzie went out with men.'

'But now your father's gone, Les, and you want me, don't you?'

Leslie nodded, unable to deny Gage the knowledge.

He moved down beside her in bed, and took her into his arms. 'I'm not going to do anything,' he said, brushing his fingers through her tousled hair and gently kissing the tip of her nose. 'This changes the entire perspective of our relationship.'

'Why?' Leslie asked, feeling frustration eat into her now.

'Because whatever we're going to have between us will be so beautiful, I don't want it marred. We have to get this thing with Fletcher Paper over first, Les. You feel that way too, don't you?'

She nodded.

'Good.' He kissed her nose. 'Do you have any ice cream?'

'Gage.' Leslie laughed, relieved that he was being so patient with her. 'Are you always eating?'

'Ice cream's a sexy food.'

She kissed his mouth impulsively, sensing an affectionate warmth between them. 'How does chocolate chip sound?'

'Fantastic.'

'Sounds better than me, huh?' she teased.

'Only if eaten in your company. Sex is a lot of things, Les. It's being here with you right now, eating with you. It's not only the act in bed.'

'Says the man of experience to his virgin bride.' Leslie stopped abruptly when she realized what she had said. Bride! To add to the confusion she said, 'I didn't mean bride in the sense — '

Gage cut her words off with a firm kiss. 'I know what you meant.' His hand strayed to pat her bottom. 'I'll go get the ice cream. Is it in your freezer?' he asked.

'Yes, and there are crystal dishes in the cupboard over the counter.'

'And silver spoons in the drawer?' Gage asked.

'Yes,' Leslie said.

'Oh, my God. Silk sheets, silver spoons. I'm gonna be spoiled.'

Leslie giggled as he left her. She got up slowly, took off her jeans and slipped into her nightgown and yellow silk robe that flowed around her ankles. She brushed her hair, noticing how bright her eyes were. Even though they hadn't made love, she felt loved. Although maybe that was being presumptuous, she thought as she replaced the hairbrush on a lace mat. Gage wanted her physically, but that didn't mean he loved her.

'Ice cream's ready,' he called from the kitchen.

'Coming,' Leslie said and, tightening the belt on the robe, joined him.

They finished two dishes of ice cream each while they talked, comparing childhoods, teenage years, school, college. Leslie had never felt so exhilarated in all her life, and yet content. She felt as if all she ever wanted was within the walls of her apartment tonight.

As their talk finally petered out, Leslie's eyelids drooped. Gage smiled. 'Tired?'

'Exhausted,' she told him.

Strong arms carried her back to the

bedroom, and Gage took off her robe and tucked her beneath her silk coverlet. 'Go to sleep,' he said.

Leslie immediately panicked. 'Don't leave,' she begged.

'I won't leave,' Gage promised, and kissed her.

★ ★ ★

Gage closed the bedroom door and walked back into the living room. He picked up their discarded dishes and rinsed them at the sink in the kitchen. Hands thrust into his pockets, he wandered around Leslie's apartment, stopping by the front door to make sure it was securely locked.

Staring out at the distant mountains and the rolling ocean, he decided that he would bide his time and take Leslie Fletcher easily. He hadn't felt this close to love for a woman since his marriage, and after many years of wariness it was probably as new to him as it was to Les. Poor kid. Paul Fletcher's protectiveness and inability to express his love had hurt his daughter. Gage wanted desperately to erase all the pain and expose the warm loving woman she was.

He sighed deeply. What if Fletcher's board turned down Les's proposal? What if he had to fight for his cause at Preston Falls?

He glanced at the bedroom door. He didn't want to hurt her, but he loved Preston Falls as well. It was better he didn't make love to her until he knew the choice he had to make. But he wanted to sleep with her, feel her close to him. He walked into the bedroom, and slipped out of his jeans.

Leslie murmured his name in her sleep as Gage eased beneath the bed covers.

'It's me,' he said quietly. 'Keep sleeping, Les.'

'Mmm.' Leslie moved closer, her white silk nightgown creeping around her thighs.

Her bare legs entwined with Gage's, and he wondered if this was a good idea, but she was reaching out to him so innocently that he couldn't deny her. Tousled and warm, she snuggled into his arms. She seemed to need him as much as he needed her. He closed his eyes.

$$\star \quad \star \quad \star$$

Leslie awoke once in the night, startled to find that she wasn't alone. Faced with Gage's tanned male back, she wanted to stroke him, to feel the ripple of muscle beneath his firm flesh. But she restrained herself, not wanting to wake him. Instead, she lay drowsily beside him, luxuriating in the heat of his body, desire not far from the surface. They would have to wait until after the board meeting to make love. Leslie only hoped that the board's answer to her request would be affirmative. She couldn't bear the thought of going through the rest of her life without Gage.

$$\star \quad \star \quad \star$$

'This bathroom is unbelievable.' Gage's voice slipped into Leslie's consciousness above the rain pounding on the windows.

She yawned and stared at the man standing at her bathroom door with one of her yellow towels wrapped around his waist.

'Why is it unbelievable?' she asked thickly.

'It's your bathtub. Is it real marble?'

'Of course.'

'Of course,' Gage mimicked. 'Leslie Fletcher, *you* are unbelievable.'

Leslie laughed, and pushed her thick brown hair from her eyes. 'You can use it if you like.'

'I already have, lady.'

'What time is it?'

'Time for you to get up and go to work. Coffee's on.'

She flopped back against the pillow. 'Are you always so cheerful in the morning?'

'Always,' he assured her.

'Then why did your wife leave you?'

'Maybe I was too cheerful.' He came and sat on the bed beside her, blue eyes gazing humorously over her sleepy body.

'Penny told me that your wife didn't like your activism,' Leslie said.

'That was an excuse for 'help, let me out.' We were young and impetuous, Les.'

'Did you love her?'

Gage took hold of her hand. 'At the time, but not anymore.' He stroked Leslie's fingers. 'Anyhow, let's talk about us. Did you sleep well?'

'Like a log, even though I had company.'

'Surprisingly, I slept too,' Gage told her. 'But I couldn't go through many nights like that without . . . '

'We could have . . . ' Leslie said softly.

Gage firmly shook his head. 'No. Wait until we know what's happening, and we have a clear field.'

Leslie sighed. 'I have a board meeting this morning, but obviously I have no proposal. If I work hard, maybe next week.'

Gage squeezed her hand, but he didn't say anything. He stood up and hitched the towel around his hips. 'I'd better get dressed.'

Leslie wished he wouldn't. Half naked, smelling of soap, his virility pronounced by the fuzz around his jaw and upper lip, she found him stimulating.

'And don't look at me like that.'

'Like what?'

'Like you could devour me.'

Leslie stretched languorously and slid out of bed, her nightgown clinging to her body. She sleepily rubbed her eyes and yawned.

'Get in the bathroom, woman,' Gage said, and gave her a helpful push.

Leslie hummed to herself as she bathed and dressed. She chose a new green dress with a matching jacket, and left her hair loose. But as she slipped her feet into black leather heels, her high spirits took a nosedive. What if her board didn't approve her report on Preston Falls? These moments with Gage suddenly became very precious and she rushed into the living room to find him sitting on her couch, sipping coffee and leafing through a magazine.

'Are you going home today?' she asked.

Gage nodded. 'Unfortunately, yes. I have an appointment later on this afternoon. I told you I was selling my business.'

'Yes, you did.' Leslie helped herself to coffee. 'So what happens when you sell it?'

'I'm not sure yet.'

Leslie glanced out the window at the misty day. 'At least it's stopped raining.'

'At least,' Gage repeated solemnly and stood up. 'I'd better get going, and let you get to the office.' He picked up his leather jacket.

Leslie followed him to the door and impulsively kissed his rough cheek. 'Thanks for staying.'

Gage's fingers traced her kiss. 'Thanks

for letting me stay. See you, Les.'

'I'll be in touch,' she told him, and watched him leave.

When she was sure he had gone, she returned to her bedroom to make the bed and brush her hair once more. She slipped into a tan raincoat, picked up her purse and briefcase and went downstairs to the waiting limousine.

* * *

Leslie spent the entire week trying to write a report that was in Fletcher's favor but with concessions to Gage and his cause. She had seen the antiquated equipment at Preston Falls with her own eyes. Gage had shown her the foamy white pollution in the streams, and the sharpness of the sulfur was everpresent on the pine-laden breeze. She understood Gage's concern, but she also understood her position as president of Fletcher Paper. It was a position that tore her apart.

She loved Gage so much that not

seeing him actually hurt physically. More than once she almost called him just to hear his deep voice. But she held off, glued to one spot by an ingrained decorum. She wished he would contact her, but she knew he felt it would be a painful meeting. Better they keep apart until they knew what direction their personal relationship could take.

Finally, Leslie asked Frank to give her some guidance with her proposal.

After reading it, by sitting silently in one of her chairs for half an hour, Frank glanced up. 'They won't go for it.'

Leslie's heart sank. 'What do you mean?'

'The board won't let Preston blackmail them into outlaying' — Frank tapped his fingers on the sheaf of papers — 'all this, for a small insignificant mill.'

'It's not insignificant, Frank.' Leslie's hands ran nervously up and down the worn amber leather arms of her chair. 'It's a place where people work under extreme pressure because of the ancient equipment, and it's a town where people live, and they're entitled to a clean water supply.'

'Preston's really got to you, hasn't he?'

'I saw it with my own eyes.'

'Okay.' Frank rested the report on her desk. 'Then you'll have to make some financial changes. What you're proposing is much too high.'

Leslie and Frank stayed up all night, or at least until the sun rose over the ocean. Leslie grabbed a limousine home and tiredly let herself into her apartment. She undressed and rolled beneath the oyster silk coverlet. Her report was ready for the board. Julie would be typing it for distribution. All Leslie wanted to do now was sleep.

The ringing telephone woke her up, and Leslie fumbled for the receiver by her bed, noticing that she had slept through an entire day. For a few pulsing moments, she hoped it might be Gage calling, but it was a woman's voice.

'Leslie Fletcher?' the voice asked.

'Yes,' Leslie said cautiously, thoughts of abduction never far from her mind.

'This is Suzie Petrone, Les.'

It took a while for Leslie's sleepy brain to register before she squealed, 'Suzie, for heaven's sake. Are you in Vancouver?'

'I'm staying with my parents. I arrived from Europe yesterday.'

'Is your family with you?'

'No.' Her friend paused. 'I'll explain all that when I see you. I really would like to see you, Les.'

'I'd like to see you too,' Leslie said sincerely. 'Would you like me to pick you up and we'll go and eat dinner — if you haven't eaten, that is.'

'No, I haven't eaten. I'd love that. Mom and Dad still live in the same house.'

'I'll be there in about an hour,' Leslie assured her friend.

Leslie showered and quickly dressed in navy slacks and a matching silk blouse. Suede jacket over her arm, she went down to the parking area to her car.

Suzie's parents lived in a two-story house in the suburbs, and Leslie parked in the wide driveway when she arrived. Suzie was waiting by the door, and the two women hugged.

'It's so good to see you.' Leslie smiled, looking at her friend, but the smile faded slightly when she saw how much Suzie had changed. Gone was the plumpness. Suzie was tanned but gaunt, her blond hair, long and streaky white, adding to her slimness.

'You look . . . ' Leslie stammered.

'Lousy,' Suzie added. 'I know. Let's get going and I'll tell you all about it.'

As Leslie drove downtown, Suzie explained her situation. 'I'm having trouble with Dominic,' she said. 'That's why I'm home here for a few weeks. I'm trying to sort things out in my mind.'

'Tell me what happened.' Leslie urged her friend to confide her unhappiness.

'Well, nothing really. He's just so strong, so macho . . . it wears me down.'

'What about the children?'

'They're with Dom. It's nothing like that, Les. He's a good father and everything, and he's a good husband if you want to be a lady of leisure and not use your brain.'

'But I thought that's what you wanted,' Leslie protested. 'You were the one who said, 'Give me a tall, strong, man and I'll have the world.''

'Did I say that?' Suzie laughed. 'I should have taken your advice. Keep away from tall, strong men. They're too much like Daddy, How is Daddy by the way?'

'He died,' Leslie said, realizing how hollow the words sounded now.

'How?' Suzie was genuinely shocked.

'He had a heart attack.'

'Who's running Fletcher Paper?'

'Me.'

'You are? Leslie, that's fantastic. You're rich, you're powerful, you're busy and occupied. I bet the men just come running.'

'Not really,' Leslie said.

'You always were so romantic, Les. You didn't like your father, but you wanted to meet a knight in shining armor just like him.'

'You met yours,' Leslie retorted.

'All that glitters isn't gold,' Suzie shot back. 'Surely you've met someone.'

Leslie smiled. 'I have. I'll tell you about him over dinner.'

They went to a little Hungarian restaurant that Leslie always enjoyed. The food was wholesome, served with dumplings and crusty bread and butter. A single candle lit each small round table.

Over the meal of chicken paprikash, Leslie let her heart out to her friend, relieved to finally unburden herself.

'Well, don't look on the dark side,' Suzie said positively. 'Your board will come through, and you can live happily ever after.'

'I'm not sure of that either.' Leslie sighed. 'Gage lives up in Preston Falls.'

'Well, you can't go live up there, can you?'

'Of course not,' Leslie said.

'Then get him to come and live in Vancouver. If he loves you, he will.'

But Leslie wasn't so sure that Suzie was right. Gage lived in Preston Falls because he didn't like the city. How could she expect him to move back to Vancouver? And why even bother thinking about these small problems when the largest barrier hadn't even been scaled?

9

The leather of her father's chair creaked as Leslie sat down to face her board on Monday morning. She probably would always think of the chair as her father's, she thought, watching male heads pore over copies of her report.

She crossed her fingers on her knee as the crinkling of turning paper began to grate on her nerves. She longed to pour more coffee, but she couldn't move from her seat. The board's acceptance of her proposal could mean an open slate to her relationship with Gage. If Gage loved her, that was. Suzie accused her of being idealistic, and she was. Love had been a long time coming, but now that it had, Leslie wanted it to be perfect.

Frank, beside her, closed his copy of the report. George Statler put one plump hand on his closed report and glanced around at the other board members. They all closed their reports.

'Leslie,' George began in a patronizing way, 'this is all very well, but a lot of added expense, don't you think?'

Leslie was prepared to defend herself. 'We're talking about the preservation of the environment here, George,' she said firmly.

Ron Statler, George's balding father, interrupted. He thumped his finger on the report. 'I think we're also talking about Fletcher Paper's best interests. We don't throw money away for nothing.'

'This isn't for nothing,' Leslie told him. 'Fletcher's equipment at Preston Falls is ancient and there are minimal pollution controls on the mill. For the past year, the water supply has been threatened.'

'We're not the only ones,' George pointed out.

'I'm well aware of that, but if we do our bit, then we can feel right about ourselves. We don't want Fletcher

Paper's image tarnished.' Leslie leaned back in her chair, pleased with herself.

Courtland Page looked agitated. 'We won't get tarnished by one little community. Come on, Leslie.'

Finlay Dawson sighed. 'She has a point, Court. This could make us look like saints.'

'No paper company is going to look like a saint.' Alan laughed.

The entire board joined nervously in his humor.

Leslie clenched her fists beneath the table. 'Maybe we should try to make ourselves look better,' she suggested.

Peter Forbes leaned forward. 'Who put you up to this?'

'I've had dealings with some of the employees of Fletcher, and the union head,' Leslie said, not wanting to mention Gage's name.

'It was probably Gage Preston,' Ray Fletcher, her uncle, said. 'Am I right?'

Frank nodded.

George Statler shook his head. 'I really don't think that Gage Preston is a good enough reason for us to lay out this kind of money right now. It's not boom time.' He laughed at his own pun on the logging industry.

Leslie ignored him, getting annoyed at the way they were playing with her. 'I think this is a very reasonable request. Preston Falls is in danger of becoming seriously polluted. If we do something about it now, we can save ourselves future trouble. It's obvious.'

'We could close the place down,' Ron said.

'No,' Leslie flung at him, and then gritted her teeth to gain control. 'We are not closing the mill. It has not been operating at a loss and we have no reason to close it.'

'So we give in to their demands,' George said. 'Just like that.' He clicked his fingers.

'Women are soft,' Donald McIntosh snorted.

Leslie glared at him. 'Don't you all care?' she asked, but she could see they didn't. They were only concerned about their small world, and that was within the steel and glass confines of the Fletcher Tower. Preston Falls, and the men who slaved to make them rich and powerful, were not important.

Frank put up his hand. 'Why don't we take a vote, Les,' he said. 'All for.'

Alan Aranson, Peter Forbes, and Ray Fletcher raised their hands.

'All against,' Frank asked.

Everyone else put up their hands.

'Abstainers.' Frank glanced around.

No hands.

'You're outvoted, Leslie,' Frank said softly.

Leslie was furious. Anger coiled inside her. It was almost as if their actions had been planned before she even presented her report — or any report, for that matter. 'Fine. I'll let Mr. Preston know your decision, but I'll rework my presentation. Maybe we can come to an agreement somewhere down the line before any militancy arises. Now, I don't think there's any more business, is there, Frank?'

'We can adjourn until next week,' Frank said.

Leslie remained seated as everyone filed out. Frank patted her hand. 'I'm sorry.'

'You did your best,' Leslie said. 'After all, you don't have a vote.'

Frank stood up and gathered his papers. 'I'll see you in your office.' He nodded to Peter Forbes, who had stayed behind, before he left.

Peter shuffled his black leather briefcase beneath his arm, looking formal in his black suit, with his thick dark hair well-groomed. 'Leslie, I'm really with you, you know.'

'I noticed, thank you,' Leslie said.

'I wasn't in the running for president. Others were.'

As the door closed, Leslie nodded at it. Now I get the picture, she thought. There was jealousy in the ranks. She stood up and pushed her papers in her briefcase. In the elevator she was still too angry to feel sadness of what was to come with Gage, but she knew she didn't want to face him. She had more or less given him the impression that she was on his side. He was probably expecting a positive result from the board meeting.

Frank was pacing her office when she arrived. She dropped her case on her desk and put her hands on the hips of her slim gray skirt. 'So what happens now?' she asked.

'Prepare another report, I suppose,' Frank said. 'You'll have to talk to Preston, and try and calm him down.'

'He might not be willing to wait any longer.' Leslie sank into her chair. 'Frank, tell me who was running for president.'

Frank pushed his hands in his pockets. 'Ron Statler, but George wouldn't have minded either.'

'Why do you think my father left it to me, Frank?'

Frank shrugged. 'You were his pride and joy, Les. He used to proudly show your picture to everyone and announce that one day you'd take over Fletcher

Paper. The others didn't have a chance.'

'He was proud of me?' Leslie's voice was shaky. Frank's news on top of her anger made her feel weak.

'He cared, Les. I know he never seemed to show it much, but he did.'

'Okay,' Leslie said. 'I can see why Ron and George are against me, but why the others?'

'Well, Peter and Alan, aren't, you know, and neither is Ray, but your father kind of sat on the others, and now they're probably letting their bitterness show by giving you a hard time. You realize that you could have been proposing new rugs for the Fletcher Tower, and they probably wouldn't have passed the motion.'

Leslie nodded. 'I thought as much.' She sighed.

Frank smiled slightly. 'We'll work something out. Don't worry.'

When Frank had gone, Leslie mulled over his words. So her father had cared about her. He had a funny way of showing it, she thought, fingering Paul

Fletcher's gold pen. He probably thought that leaving her the Fletcher legacy was proof enough.

Don't worry, Frank had said. Leslie buried her head in her hands. Frank didn't have to face Gage.

* * *

Leslie spent the rest of the day with Gage's phone numbers in front of her on the desk. As she worked, she would look at them, her hands sometimes half moving to the telephone but then stopping as if pulled back by a magnet.

Finally, just before five, she called the Preston Falls number. Relieved when she received no answer, she hung up and tried the Vancouver one, not expecting to get any answer there either.

'Hello,' Gage's voice said.

'It's you,' she said stupidly.

'Les?'

'I didn't know you'd be in the city.'

'Then why phone the number?'

230

'Because I tried Preston Falls first.'

'I had some business to attend to, so I flew in yesterday afternoon and spent some time with my family.'

So Gage had been in town yesterday. Leslie felt despondent because he hadn't contacted her, but she hid her gloom as she spoke. 'My proposal went to the board today.'

'And?' Gage asked curtly.

'I can't tell you over the phone. Could we meet at my apartment?'

'That bad, huh?'

'I just want to explain everything in detail so you'll understand,' Leslie rushed on. 'If you do want to throw something, it's better in private.'

He laughed harshly. 'Thanks.'

'Come for dinner,' she offered impulsively, longing to see him even if it might be the last time.

'I will,' he said. 'I know what you have to say, but I'd like to see you.'

Gage hung up abruptly, and Leslie brushed her hair from her forehead as she broke out into a sudden sweat. The hard edge she detected in Gage's voice was a bad omen.

To sweeten her meeting with Gage, Leslie left the office early to go home to prepare dinner. When the beef kebabs and sweet and sour sauce were prepared alongside a lush green salad, she took a shower and dressed in a bright yellow jumpsuit that belied her mood. She brushed out her hair, leaving it tousled and curly around her features. Her face showed the strain of the day, but she managed to hide any shadows with makeup.

As she waited for Gage, Leslie opened a bottle of light red wine, wondering why she hadn't just told him the news on the telephone. But she knew that mixed with the trepidation at what she had to tell Gage was the thrill of seeing him again.

Love couldn't be denied, she realized as her heart thumped in anticipation for his arrival. When she saw him at last, her eyes followed his navy slacks and shirt beneath his black leather jacket, and her body flowed with heat. His blue eyes were wary as she took his jacket to hang it carefully in the closet.

She rested her fingers against the leather for a moment, dragging out the warmth of his body and inhaling his scent. She wanted to curl up with pain and cry.

But Leslie was used to hiding her feelings. She turned from the closet with a wide smile. 'So how are you?'

'Cut the phoniness, Les,' Gage said. 'I've missed you, but I thought I should keep out of your way.'

Leslie hadn't expected him to be so blatantly honest. But then the last time they had been together, they had shared a night in her bed. She supposed that gave him the right to be blunt with her. Should she admit that she had also missed him? Or would that be showing too much of her feelings? After all, in a few minutes, their whole relationship could be in tatters. To protect herself, she said, 'I've been busy.'

'I thought as much.' He stuffed his

hands in his pockets and sniffed the air. 'So what smells so good?'

'Beef kebabs.' Leslie was glad he had changed the subject. 'Do you want to eat?'

'That's half of why I'm here.'

Leslie showed him to the intimate nook by the window where she had set the table with tall crystal wine glasses and silver cutlery on bright orange cotton mats.

As usual Gage ate everything Leslie put in front of him, enjoying his food to the utmost. Leslie was pleased she had made kebabs. She was able to pick at the small pieces without looking as if she weren't eating. When they had finished, she served the coffee on the table by the sofa. But neither of them sat down.

Gage stared broodingly at the panoramic view. 'Okay, spill,' he said when she handed him his coffee cup. 'I've come to the conclusion, by now, that the board turned down your presentation.'

'How astute.' Leslie laughed nervously.

'Do you want to tell me why?'

Leslie wished that his features weren't so achingly familiar. She drew in a deep breath. 'Apparently, some of the board members are jealous because I was made president.'

'What's that got to do with Preston Falls?'

'They would have turned down any proposal I made to them, Gage.'

Gage put down his full cup of coffee. 'Could I see a copy of your report?'

'It's confidential. I'm sorry.'

'Okay, then tell me what you put in it.'

'I outlined a proposal for new equipment for the mill, incorporating pollution controls.'

'What did the board object to?'

'They used the financial cost as the excuse.'

Gage's blue eyes pinned Leslie down. 'And of course you fought back?'

'Yes,' Leslie said jerkily, hating to be the subject of his interrogation.

'You had no reason not to fight back?'

Leslie swallowed hard. 'What are you getting at?'

'You could have made the report financially high intentionally to gain the board's favor.'

Leslie was immediately incensed at his slander. 'You'd believe that of me?'

'Well, I did think you were on my side,' he snapped.

'I'm on Fletcher's side, but I believe in your cause.'

'Sure, you do.' Gage waved his hand at their finished meal. 'You sit here eating a gourmet meal, served on bone china, when there are people in Preston Falls eating fish that's poisoned by your company.'

Leslie forced back the hot tears that pressed behind her eyes. 'So what am I supposed to do? Go and get myself poisoned? You don't exactly live a life without luxury.'

Gage sighed. 'Okay, that was a nasty shot, but I've been hanging around, wasting time, waiting for you to get a handle on this thing. I've been angry for a long time about what's happening up at Preston Falls. It festers inside me that little people get hurt because a company like Fletcher has all the power. I can't wait any longer. If you want trouble, then you're going to get trouble.'

'I can go to the board again,' Leslie told him.

'Just so they can say no once more. Why bother?'

'I did my best,' Leslie protested. 'If you'd been there, you would have heard me defend your cause.'

'If you'd done your best, you would be giving me good news tonight, instead of bad. We would be making love instead of arguing.'

Tears squeezed from Leslie's velvet brown eyes.

Gage masked his expression. 'And don't give me tears. You're the president of a company. I'm no male chauvinist. If your father had done this to me, I'd be just as mad.'

'But you didn't get anywhere with my father.' Leslie wanted to give him back some of the upsetting words he was giving her. 'And you know why? Because he wasn't a woman. He couldn't fall for your handsome face and your charming words.'

But Gage had an answer for her. 'I never faced your father across a desk because I tried to negotiate in a civilized manner. Obviously, the Fletchers don't know the meaning of the word.'

'So what are you going to do?' Leslie held her breath.

'I'll go through with the action I threatened,' Gage said coolly. He glanced around. 'Where did you hide my jacket?'

Leslie walked to the closet on shaky legs and took out his jacket. She handed it to him, and he slung it over his shoulder. She wondered when she'd ever seen patience and understanding, and maybe love, in his features. He looked ruthless and hard, just like Paul Fletcher. The similarity, the rejection, the realization that it was now over with Gage, were almost too much for Leslie to bear. She reached out and gripped the back of her velvet couch.

Gage moved to the door. He sighed deeply and shook his head as if what he was doing didn't please him. 'Thanks for the dinner, Les. I guess all that sugar you put in my coffee didn't help, because I forgot to drink it.'

As Leslie stared at the closed door and heard the buzz of the elevator, her heart cramped. For one moment, she almost ran after him, to beg forgiveness and a second chance, but she stopped herself. Whenever she had run after her father, she had been rewarded with a cold gray glance and a flick of the wrist. She couldn't handle that type of putdown again. Her pain over Gage was excrutiating.

She glanced around her apartment. Was Gage right? Was her lifestyle so grand that she had no touch with reality? She didn't believe it was true. She had been born into this wealth, but underneath she was scared and vulnerable.

'Oh, Gage,' she murmured tearfully, sinking to her knees on the thick ivory rug.

She had never cried so hard in her life. When the last of the wracking sobs subsided, she lay on her back, exhausted but calm. Not only had she lost her first round at the board meeting, but she had also lost the only man she had ever loved.

★   ★   ★

Gage's silence was ominous. Three weeks passed without word of militant action from Preston Falls. Leslie lived on the edge of her nerves, waiting for the bomb to drop.

Frank was jubilant because of Gage's silence.

'I told you he was nothing to worry about,' he told Leslie after a Monday morning board meeting. 'He was a small fish in a smaller pond. A lot of smoke, but no fire.'

'Oh, cut the clichés, Frank.' Leslie grew impatient as she gathered papers into her briefcase. She had been working herself in circles, trying to keep Gage out of her mind. She had never thought that love would be this painful. The days were relatively peaceful, but her nights were turbulent. Lack of sleep was manifesting itself in the shadows beneath her eyes and loss of weight. Instead of shopping for new clothes, because she had no initiative to do so, she tightened belts and moved buttons, hoping she didn't look like an under-nourished scarecrow.

The only thing that pleased her was that she had never let Gage know in words that she loved him. It was obvious to her now that he had been using her. He'd almost said as much that last night they were together, when he'd told her that he'd been waiting for her to get used to being president.

Leslie supposed that he had thought he might have a little amusement out of the waiting. What a shock he must have had when he found her to be a virgin. No wonder he didn't touch her. At least he had some scruples — he probably knew that she would want a commitment from him if they went to bed.

But however much she despised Gage's ruthless behavior, she couldn't stop loving him. She now understood her mother's motives with her father. Caroline Fletcher was right. Whatever happened, the love didn't stop.

10

Gage sat around the table with Peter Slater and Arne Haywood, the shop steward from the mill. As he listened to their conversation, he realized that he finally had them convinced to take a vote from the union for a strike at the Preston Falls paper mill. But although he still believed fully in his cause, he felt that it had backfired on him. Life without Leslie was a barren desert.

He understood Peter and Arne's position. Neither could afford to jeopardize the jobs at the mill, but a nasty accident the day before yesterday and the diagnosis of mercury poisoning in one of the mill worker's children had finally convinced them that strike action was inevitable if they were to get new equipment and a cleaner environment.

'So what do you think, Gage?' Peter asked.

Gage smiled crookedly. He'd missed the last lap of the conversation.

Peter glanced pointedly at the two empty scotch glasses in front of Gage while he and Arne were only drinking draft beer, but he didn't mention anything. He sighed. 'We'll take a vote on Friday afternoon, and if everyone is in agreement we'll begin with a number of rotating, one-day strikes.'

'We'll ask the workers to bring along their families, just to make the point clearer to management. This is a town problem,' Arne said.

'It's what I've been working toward,' Gage told him.

'Good.' Arne got to his feet. 'Thanks for the beer, Peter. See you, Gage.'

Gage watched the young man walk out of the gloomy beer parlor, then he glanced at Peter.

'So what's up?' Peter asked.

Gage turned his two empty glasses around on the table. 'I was hoping that

Fletcher would come through over the last few weeks.'

'You mean you aren't really in favor of striking?'

'Yes and no,' Gage said. 'The problem is, Peter, that woman got to me.'

'I thought so,' Peter said gently. 'I could see the way you were reacting to her when you came to dinner that night. She's a good-looking lady and I liked her, but you can't let your personal feelings get in the way of this, Gage. You know that. You've given her a chance, and she didn't come through. It's obvious that Fletcher Paper won't budge without a rebellion.'

'You were the one who was cautious before,' Gage reminded his friend.

'Well, you know it's always been more than just the environment with me, Gage. We have to have safer working conditions, and John's accident proves it. But when the kids start getting sick, and I think of my own kids and my future grandchildren, I'm with you all the way. I can represent Fletcher Paper and fight for the employees, but you can fight for the town because the people have confidence in you.' Peter drained his beer glass. 'You can't pull out now, Gage.'

'I'm not going to pull out,' Gage promised.

★   ★   ★

'They're on strike up in Preston Falls.' Frank met Leslie on the way into her office on Tuesday morning.

'When did you find out?' she asked, taking off the brown cord jacket that matched her skirt.

'A while ago. Apparently, it's just for one day, but the whole town is marching around with placards and yelling slogans. Some guy got his arm crushed last week in the machinery, and some kid has mercury poisoning or something. They're all fighting mad.'

Leslie sighed. 'I told you Gage Preston meant business. So what do we do now?'

'Go up to Preston Falls and talk to the management and Gage Preston. Get them to stop and we'll negotiate reasonably.'

'Do you think the board will negotiate reasonably?' Leslie emphasized the last two words.

'They'll have to,' Frank said. 'We can't afford strikes.'

Leslie put her hands on her hips. 'They should have thought of that before. I bet the board didn't really think that Gage would go through with it, did they?'

'Well, he's just a two-bit log salvager.'

'He's a man with a cause, and the union on his side,' Leslie reminded Frank. 'Okay, let's jump into action. I'll go up to Preston Falls and see what's happening with my own eyes. I'll try and persuade Gage to wait for another presentation to the board.'

'I'll come with you,' Frank said. 'When do you want to go?'

'Today.'

A chartered plane flew Frank and

Leslie to Preston Falls. The pilot was a seasoned bushman who liked to talk. Leslie much preferred Gage's strong hands piloting her planes, and was relieved when they landed in Preston Falls. She noticed that Frank went a little white when the plane gave the impression of landing in the river, and it vividly reminded Leslie of her first trip with Gage. But she had to hide her aching heart as they were met by an agitated Cliff Daniels.

'Money's more important than causes,' Cliff said as he drove Frank and Leslie through the town of Preston Falls to the mill. 'They'll come back to work.'

'Frank was telling me about some accident?' Leslie questioned.

'Someone got his arm crushed, and everyone's running to the doctor thinking they've got mercury poisoning. They're mad, all right.'

'They look it,' Frank commented as Cliff slowed the car through a crowd of angry protesters. An egg crushed and splattered against the window beside

Leslie and she automatically ducked as Cliff accelerated. At last they were rushed into the paper mill and Cliff's office.

Leslie wasn't surprised to see Peter Slater there, but she hadn't expected Gage. He stood up from his chair as Leslie entered with Cliff and Frank, and gave her an assessing blue stare.

But Leslie was determined to make this a friendly meeting. She smiled. 'Gage Preston. I don't believe you've met Frank Lehman, my personal advisor.'

The two men shook hands, and then Frank shook with Peter, whom he already knew.

Cliff made sure they were all comfortably seated and served with coffee. Outside the open window the strikers grew quieter.

It was the first time Leslie had attended a meeting to try and stop a strike, and she was glad of Frank's experience. Frank could act as mediator, while Cliff and Leslie represented management; Peter, the union; and Gage, the people.

She found that there were no raised voices, but each man had his cause, his reason for attending the meeting and no one was going to budge. By the end of the afternoon, it was back to Leslie to write a second report to her board. Tuesday's strike was also over and the town was peaceful again.

'Does this mean that you'll hold off the strikes?' Leslie asked, looking around at the men.

Peter shook his head. 'No. We've started now, and we'll continue until we have something in writing.'

'So you're as militant as your friend, Gage.' Leslie tried for a bit of humor to brighten the oncoming evening.

'We both believe in what we're doing,' Gage interjected coolly.

'So we've gathered from today's meeting.' Cliff stood up. 'Why don't we all go and get some dinner?'

Leslie didn't expect Gage to accompany them to the marina café, but he did. Now that the meeting was over the conversation became more general, and Leslie became completely aware of Gage as a man, not a business opponent.

He was wearing a navy suit that she hadn't seen before and it fitted him immaculately. Over dinner, he loosened his tie a couple of notches to display his tanned throat. He stood out among the other men with a power Leslie couldn't quite pin down. Or was it just that she loved Gage, and the others were merely acquaintances?

As she picked at her fruit salad dessert, Gage's blue eyes met hers, and for a moment they were unguarded, open and warm. Her love, needing crumbs, made her smile at him, but his eyes had now gone cold.

It was dark when they left the café.

'Are you staying over, or going back to Vancouver tonight?' Cliff asked Frank.

'We have a plane waiting at the airport,' Frank said.

'I'm going that way, so I'll give you a ride over,' Gage suggested.

The last thing Leslie really wanted was to be squashed between Frank and Gage on the front seat of Gage's truck. But here she was, bumping in time with the ruts in Preston Falls's roads, her thigh pressed into Gage's.

Leslie noticed that Frank didn't say much, and she knew that he hated anything but smooth-riding limousines. Gage drove casually, one hand on the steering wheel, his elbow resting on the open window.

Leslie's hair blew in the breeze, and she wished that Frank weren't with them. She would have asked Gage to drive on. Foolishly, she might even have gone to his cottage and made love with him because she wanted to know what it was like. Instead, the floodlights from the airport strip made her lower her eyes.

Their pilot was waiting with the plane's engines warming. Frank boarded immediately, eager to return to Vancouver.

Leslie turned to Gage. 'Thank you for the lift,' she said.

'You're welcome. I hope this second proposal will be successful.'

'I hope so too.' Leslie straightened her briefcase and purse beneath her arm.

Gage's mouth firmed into a little smile. 'I enjoyed watching you today in the meeting. You're doing well, Leslie Fletcher, president.'

'I'm doing my best,' she said, recalling that she had told him that once before.

'I know,' he agreed, this time not denying it.

Then Gage did something that made her ache. He cupped her face in his warm hands. Leslie closed her eyes, his touch making her lean against him. His body was rock hard, full of heat. She longed for him, and opened her eyes to meet his, knowing he could probably see the love that spilled from her.

He shook his head, and she felt the brush of his jaw on her temple before he dropped his hands. 'I guess we'll be hearing from you?'

Leslie nodded, too choked up to speak. Gage helped her into the plane, his fingers guiding her hand, her arm, her waist. She stumbled into her seat beside Frank.

'Anything wrong, Les?' Frank asked anxiously.

'I'm fine.' Leslie turned to look out of the plane window.

Gage was walking to his truck, his broad shoulders slightly slumped. When he looked back, Leslie raised her hand in a salute, but she knew he couldn't see.

★ ★ ★

Leslie worked all hours with Frank to draft up a second report for the board. But it was a race against time as the Fletcher Paper mill at Preston Falls stopped the one-day strikes to launch a full-scale strike. The media had caught up with the affair, and they were all making news.

Gage got his fair share of airtime, and Leslie had to admit that when watching and listening to him, she couldn't help not take his side. He was lucid and sincere, and he very definitely knew what he wanted. He was becoming a national hero. Fletcher Paper was the enemy.

On Wednesday morning, Leslie's chauffeur drove her around the back of the Fletcher Tower because half the residents of Preston Falls and anyone else who believed in their cause were sprawled over the front steps.

'Blast,' Leslie muttered, gathering her belongings to rush from the limousine. She found Frank in her office. 'How's the report coming, Frank?' she asked, throwing everything haphazardly onto her desk.

'Julie's photocopying it,' Frank told her. 'I've called an emergency board meeting.'

'Good.' Leslie straightened her gray silk dress and took a deep breath. She was going to need all her wits about her today.

As Leslie entered the board room and took her place in her chair, she realized that she wasn't in awe of the men anymore. Gage's actions had thrown her headfirst into her job as president, and it had gotten her over any initial apprehension. So far she was still swimming.

'Frank is passing around the second report on Preston Falls,' she said. 'You'll notice that I've been more circumspect financially this time so I hope you'll all bestow your approval. We lose more financially by allowing the strikes than by putting new equipment and pollution controls on the mill.'

Leslie let the men rustle through the report. There were a few questions, but none that Leslie couldn't answer immediately. No one liked the militant action coming to Vancouver, or the adverse media coverage. When the vote came, Leslie had the majority.

★　★　★

By the end of the day, even though she was tired, Leslie knew she wouldn't be able to sleep if she returned to her apartment. Instead, she called Suzie and arranged to meet for dinner.

Suzie, she learned, had realized that she couldn't live without Dominic. She was returning to Italy on Sunday.

'Believe it or not,' — Suzie smiled — 'I didn't like it on my own.'

Leslie had to agree. She had always thought she knew loneliness, but since Gage it had magnified.

She was also sad to say goodbye to Suzie, but the two women promised to keep in touch more often in the future.

Near the end of the week, after the union had approved the report, Gage phoned. 'I just want to say thank you,' he said sincerely.

'I believed in what you were doing.' Leslie had to be honest.

'Thanks. What are you doing this Sunday?'

Oh, so now that it was all over he was going to pick up from where they had left off. Leslie's back went up immediately. She might love him, but she wasn't going to be used whenever he felt the whim.

'I'm busy Sunday,' she told him. 'It's my birthday, and I'm spending the day with my mother.'

Gage must have heard the coolness in her voice because he just said, 'Okay, then fine. Thanks once more.'

'All in a day's work,' Leslie said casually as she hung up. She swallowed back the threatening tears. She wasn't going to cry over Gage Preston anymore. She would slot him with her father — in the past.

Sunday was a hot sunny day that turned spring suddenly into summer. Leslie drove up to her mother's house early, not wanting to stick around home in case Gage got it into his head to phone her again. She knew she would fall into his arms if she saw him, and forgive all the harsh words that had passed between them. He had made his choice and he'd let her drop for his cause. Gage had intentionally sought her out when her father had died; he'd ruthlessly moved in on her vulnerability. He had felt some attraction for her, but it might be no more than he felt for other women. He could probably live without her. Whether she could live without him was another matter, but she was sure going to try. She had battled her father and won; she had battled her board of directors and won. She was the president of Fletcher Paper and proud of it. Gage Preston might have had her down for a few weeks, but she managed to cope.

She stopped her car, but as she pulled on the parking brake she let out a long despairing sigh. It was going to be terribly hard to keep a grip on her emotions.

★   ★   ★

'You look so thin, Les,' her mother said as they ate the salad lunch Betty served on the patio.

'I've had a lot to worry about lately.' Leslie dismissed lightly, poking her fork in the lettuce, not at all hungry.

'What a fiasco. I watched it all on TV. Why don't you take a vacation?' Caroline suggested. 'I'll go along with you.'

'I can't leave the office,' Leslie said. 'But don't let me stop you from going.'

'You won't. I've already made the plans. Australia, here I come.'

'Australia?' Leslie glanced at her mother, forgetting her own problems for a moment.

'I've always wanted to visit there,' Caroline said. 'It's one place your father didn't take me, and I have a cousin there I haven't seen for years.'

'Well, that sounds good,' Leslie told her sincerely. 'I hope you have fun.'

'I'm really excited. It's given me a new lease on life. I'll let you see the brochures later, but first let me give you your birthday present.' Caroline got up and walked into the house.

Leslie watched her, thinking that her

mother looked quite spry in a new blue silk dress.

Caroline returned with a long narrow gift, wrapped in silver paper and matching ribbon.

Leslie was delighted with the slim gold watch that looked perfect on her wrist. 'Thanks, Mom.' She kissed her mother's cheek. 'Mine went on the blink a couple of weeks ago.'

'That's what Frank said,' Caroline admitted. 'He's fed up with you asking the time every five minutes.'

Leslie smiled. 'Frank doesn't miss much.'

'He figures you're getting along really well.'

'Coming from Frank, that's quite a compliment,' Leslie said.

Her mother held her eyes. 'He also told me about Gage Preston.'

Leslie stood up to walk restlessly to the edge of the still-covered swimming pool.

Caroline joined her. 'So what's happening with Gage?'

'It's all over,' Leslie said airily.

'Well, your business association is. Frank didn't know you'd been seeing Gage privately.'

'Did you tell him?'

'No, of course not, dear.' Caroline put her hand on her daughter's arm. 'Frank doesn't need to know personal things like that. Was Gage using you?'

'I'm not sure.' Leslie felt close to tears. She was so emotional. Maybe a trip to Australia was what *she* needed, but there was so much to do at the office that she couldn't see her way clear to leave right now.

'Haven't you seen him since the situation at Preston Falls was settled?'

'He called to say thanks.'

'Doesn't he want to see you?'

'Oh, Mom, don't bug me about him.'

Caroline sighed. 'I'm not bugging you. I just want to know what I'm dealing with, Les. You've got shadows beneath your eyes like bruises, and those navy slacks look two sizes too big and your blouse is hanging on you. And don't tell me that you miss your father, because I won't believe you.'

'I do miss Dad,' Leslie admitted.

'We both do, but I'm beginning to recover, and you look like death warmed over.'

Leslie shook her head. 'I fell in love with Gage, that's all.'

Caroline looked skeptical. 'That's a lot for you, Leslie.'

'I'll get over him,' Leslie said bravely, wanting to end the conversation.

'Oh, I wish you'd come on that trip,' Caroline fussed.

But that was the last of the fussing and probing questions. Leslie stayed at the house for the remainder of the afternoon, and shared a light dinner with her mother before returning home.

Instead of going to her apartment, she parked her car at English Bay Beach and walked down to the edge of the Pacific Ocean. The sun was disappearing over the horizon, leaving pink fingers tipping the waves. It reminded her of the night she had met

Gage here, and the ice cream they had shared. It all seemed a dream now, but at least she knew what it was like to experience love. She also knew what it was like not to have that love returned — when she ached and longed for a man.

To stop herself getting melancholy, Leslie went home. But as she left the elevator at her penthouse, she felt another presence in the hallway. Blinking in the bright light, she saw Gage leaning negligently against her front door.

Leslie couldn't speak as her eyes took in his muscular body in jeans and light blue sweater. Was he thinner, or was it her imagination? He seemed a little gaunt around the cheeks, his eyes hollow.

Did he think she was thinner? Did he notice how her navy slacks sagged around her hips, and that her white silk shirt wasn't as tight around her breasts anymore? She was glad she had washed her hair this morning because it was curly and full.

She raised her velvet brown eyes to Gage's blue ones. 'Hi,' she said, feeling that one of them should speak.

'Hi,' Gage repeated, his voice husky. 'I know you said you were busy today, but you had to come home sometime.'

'How do you know I'm alone?'

'Where're you hiding your friend? In your purse?'

Leslie smiled slightly, feeling an edge of hysteria rise inside. She opened her small navy clutch purse and drew out her door key. 'No. I'm alone.'

'May I talk to you?' Gage asked.

Leslie didn't really want to let him in to her apartment. It would be her downfall to be alone with him. She had no fight left. She would let him seduce her.

'I can't talk to you out here.' Gage prodded her hesitation.

'Okay,' she agreed, and opened the door. She switched on the light, flooding the intimate ivory and apricot interior with a golden glow.

Gage followed and placed a large

brown paper bag on one of her chairs.

Leslie eyed the parcel curiously, but didn't comment. She tossed her purse and keys on a table. 'So what do you want now? Have you got another cause you want to fight?'

'Just one,' Gage said.

Leslie crossed her arms and walked away from his stifling presence. She had to be strong, and it made her hard. 'Are we going to play again?' she asked. 'How about the same routine. Ice cream on Friday night — well, we've missed that. We've missed the Saturday night date as well. So I guess it's a little warmup on Sunday evening, and slam bam I get the goods on Monday morning.'

'Stop it.' Gage moved toward her. 'It's nothing like that, Les.'

'And don't call me Les.'

'I've hurt you,' Gage said softly.

'You're darn right, you've hurt me,' she hurled at him. 'I'm just lucky I didn't sleep with you. What happened there, Gage? Did you chicken out? Did

Leslie Fletcher get a little fragile to handle when you found out that she was a virgin, or was it a big laugh?'

Gage grabbed her arms and held her still. 'Don't do that to yourself.' His blue eyes were unmasked and anxious as they scanned her features. 'I didn't want to do this to you, Leslie.'

'Then what did you intend to do?' she demanded.

'I didn't intend anything. I didn't know we'd end up feeling like this.'

'Why do you keep saying we?' Leslie tugged away from him, and wrapped her arms around her body to stop the pain from exploding.

'Because I feel the same way, Les.'

'How could you?' she flung at him. 'You made the choice between me and Preston Falls.'

'I had to, don't you understand. I've spent my life in those woods, as my family did before me. I didn't want them ruined just so you can bathe in a marble tub.'

'There you go again, slamming my

lifestyle. If you don't like it, get out, Mr. Preston. I can do without you. After all, I'm rich, I'm powerful, I can get any man . . .'

They stared at each other; brown eyes brimming with tears, blue eyes pleading.

Gage said quietly, 'Get, but not love, Leslie. There's a big difference.'

Through the mist of her tears, Leslie saw Gage's rough-hewn features, his curly dark blond hair that she knew was so soft to touch. Would she be a fool to let him go and not forgive?

'And they wouldn't love you as much as I love you,' Gage went on thickly. 'Darling Leslie, forgive me for having to choose like that, but please understand.'

His words gradually sank in. 'You love me?'

'In a way I've never loved anyone in my life. This separation has been just as painful for me, Les. I've been torn in two between doing what's right for my town, and loving you.'

'Why didn't you say?'

'I don't think I really knew how deeply I loved you until I thought I'd lost you. I was trying to keep my feelings apart from the problem at hand.'

Now that one large barrier was down, the little ones came to haunt Leslie. 'It still won't work,' she told him. 'We're from different worlds.'

'I don't think so,' Gage said. 'It's pretty much the same with lakes and rivers, oceans and beaches, the sun, the sky. That's all that matters, sweetheart.'

Leslie ran her hands up the sides of her slacks. What did he expect? she wondered. Did he want her for an affair? She loved him far too much to have him once in a while.

But it wasn't easy to think with him so close. Not being able to help herself, she rested her cheek against his hard chest, and ran her fingers up and down his sweater. He put his arms around her. 'Just you and me,' he said.

His mouth covered hers hungrily, and she responded by slipping her arms around his neck and thrusting her fingers into his curly hair.

'Tell me you love me,' he groaned against her trembling lips.

'I love you,' Leslie whispered, because he had made himself just as vulnerable to her with the same admission.

He hugged her and buried his mouth in her soft hair. 'Why are you holding back then?'

'How can you tell?'

'I can tell, Leslie. What is it?'

'I can't have an affair with you, Gage.'

Gage laughed, the sound rumbling through their bodies. 'Did I ask for an affair? I'm asking for marriage. No less.'

Gage felt her stiffen slightly. 'Now what?'

'I can't marry you either.'

'But you have to,' Gage said desperately, his blue eyes burning through her.

'I can't live in Preston Falls.'

He chuckled, relieved. 'Every move you make makes me realize why your father was so sure of you. You don't leave any rock unturned. Who's asking you to live in Preston Falls? I wouldn't expect it of you. I got a good deal on the sale of my business, and we're going to buy a house just outside of Vancouver, within commuting distance for you, and I'm going to write my book while you go on being president of Fletcher Paper.'

Leslie's heart soared with happiness. 'But what will you do with your cottage?'

'What do you want me to do with it?' Gage asked, his own happiness shining in his eyes.

'Keep it,' Leslie said. 'I'd like to spend our honeymoon there.'

'Whatever the president says.' Gage laughed.

'I can't believe you'd do all this for me.' Leslie gave him an impulsive kiss on the cheek.

'I'd do anything in the world for you. Just ask me.'

Leslie mischievously eyed the parcel he had put on her chair. 'What's in there?'

Gage grinned, and reluctantly let her go. Picking up the bag he opened it, and dipped in his fingers. 'First this.' Gage handed Leslie a black velvet ring box.

She opened it quickly, her heart beating fast. A single solitaire sapphire, the color of the ocean, shone up at her. 'It's beautiful, Gage.' Leslie lifted the ring from the box. 'Put it on for me.'

Gage took the ring and held it in the air. 'You haven't said you'll marry me yet.'

'Of course I'll marry you. I love you. I've never loved anyone else, Gage.'

'Good.' Smiling, Gage fitted the ring on Leslie's finger. 'Fit's perfectly, thanks to your mother.'

'You've been in touch with my mother?'

'Your mother is a very nice lady.' Gage took Leslie back into his arms.

'No wonder she was asking me questions today,' Leslie said, but was cut off from speaking further as Gage's mouth sealed their commitment with a kiss.

When they parted, Leslie still eyed the bulging parcel. 'What else is in there?' she asked.

'That's for after,' Gage said.

'After what?'

'After I make mad passionate love to you.' He lowered his arms and lifted her.

'But I won't be perfectly content until you tell me,' Leslie protested, her own arms sliding around his strong neck.

He nuzzled her nose. 'Okay, how about birthday cake, ice cream and hot fudge sauce.'

'That I'd believe.' Leslie laughed and snuggled closer.

As they moved toward her bedroom, Leslie said a little thank you to Paul Fletcher, and the legacy that had given her Gage Preston.

We do hope that you have enjoyed reading this large print book.

Did you know that all of our titles are available for purchase?

We publish a wide range of high quality large print books including:
Romances, Mysteries, Classics
General Fiction
Non Fiction and Westerns

Special interest titles available in large print are:
The Little Oxford Dictionary
Music Book, Song Book
Hymn Book, Service Book

Also available from us courtesy of Oxford University Press:
Young Readers' Dictionary
(large print edition)
Young Readers' Thesaurus
(large print edition)

For further information or a free brochure, please contact us at:
Ulverscroft Large Print Books Ltd.,
The Green, Bradgate Road, Anstey,
Leicester, LE7 7FU, England.
Tel: (00 44) **0116 236 4325**
Fax: (00 44) **0116 234 0205**

VISIONS OF THE HEART

Christine Briscomb

When property developer Connor Grant contracted Natalie Jensen to landscape the grounds of his large country house near Ashley in South Australia, she was ecstatic. But then she discovered he was acquiring — and ripping apart — great swathes of the town. Her own mother's house and the hall where the drama group met were two of his targets. Natalie was desperate to stop Connor's plans — but she also had to fight the powerful attraction flowing between them.

FINGALA, MAID OF RATHAY

Mary Cummins

On his deathbed, Sir James Mont-
gomery of Rathay asks his daughter,
Fingala, to swear that she will not
honour her marriage contract until
her brother Patrick, the new heir,
returns from serving the King.
Patrick must marry. Rathay must
not be left without a mistress. But
Patrick has fallen in love with the
Lady Catherine Gordon whom the
King, James IV, has given in
marriage to the young man who
claims to be Richard of York, one of
the princes in the Tower.

ZABILLET OF THE SNOW

Catherine Darby

For Zabillet, a young peasant girl growing up in the tiny French village of Fromage in the mid-fourteenth century, a respectable marriage is the height of her parents' ambitions for her. But life is changing. Zabillet's love for a handsome shepherd is tested when she is invited to join the La Neige household, where her mistress, Lady Petronella, has plans for her grandson, Benet. And over all broods the horror of the Great Death that claims all whom it touches.

PERILOUS JOURNEY

Caroline Joyce

After the execution of Charles I, Louisa's Royalist father considers it too dangerous for her to stay in England and arranges for her to go to the Isle of Man with Armand de la Tremouille, the nephew of the island's Royalist Governor. Their ship is boarded by Parliamentarians who plan to sail for Ireland, but a storm causes them to be shipwrecked on the Calf of Man. Magnus Stapleton, the Parliamentarian chief, becomes infatuated with Louisa, but she has fallen in love with Armand.

THE GYPSY'S RETURN

Sara Judge

After the death of her cruel father, Amy Keene's stepbrother and stepsister treated her just as badly. Amy had two friends, old Dr. Hilland and the washerwoman, Rosalind, with her fatherless child Becky. When Rosalind falls ill, Amy is entrusted with a letter to be given to Becky on her marriage. When the letter's contents are discovered, it causes Amy both mental and physical suffering and sets the seal of fate upon Rosalind's gypsy friend, Elias Jones.

WEB OF DECEIT

Margaret McDonagh

A good-looking man turned up on Louise's doorstep one day, introducing himself as Daniel Kinsella, an Australian friend of her brother-in-law, Greg. He said he had come to stay whilst he did some research — apparently Greg had written to her about it. Louise's initial reaction was to turn him away, but he was very persuasive. However, she was to discover that Daniel had bluffed his way into her life, and soon she found herself caught up in his dangerous mission.